the
Fight

Taylor S. Joseph

★ ★ ★ ★
Four Star Publishing
Canton, Michigan

Published by:
Four Star Publishing
P.O. Box 871784
Canton, MI 48187
fourstarpublishing@comcast.net

ISBN: 978-0-9815894-5-9

Book design by Lee Lewis Walsh, Words Plus Design,
www.wordsplusdesign.com

Printed in the United States of America

part one

the view from heaven

They say that the battle for a man's soul starts behind the glorious gates of heaven and in the deepest, darkest depths of hell on the day he is born. A soul is the most coveted prize in both places; so coveted that it is said that a war ensues every time a soul's fate is in question, greater than the worst war ever experienced on earth.

Behind heaven's magnificent gates, an announcement rang out, "Sector seventeen level two angel, report to your superiors." The breeze blew lightly and the light in heaven was bright and calming. Each cloud was lined in silver and gold. It was the greatest place in the universe, with all its inhabitants working together for the good of mankind.

The angel Andrew turned to his assistant, Phillip, and said, "I wonder what that's about. All the assignments have been given out already."

"Maybe it's about a promotion to sector eighteen," Phillip said. "You have been working very hard lately. The load was heavy this year and you planned all the assignments well."

"I hope you're right," Andrew said.

Andrew wore a white robe with gold trim, as they all did in heaven. His face glowed with serenity; like everyone else there, his angelic form resembled his human body at the time of his death. He had died at the age of fifty-six, having lived in Europe in the fifteenth century. Andrew had been a stable hand when he was young and eventually became a blacksmith. He had lived his entire life as an honest man, never taking advantage of people in need, and showing much compassion for the poor and the homeless. His never-ending kindness and commitment to God had earned him a place in the glorious kingdom of heaven. He was a true fighter for men's souls.

Andrew's superior, William, had been an uncompromising man who lived in the fourteenth century, and now he was a dedicated angel. He had died at the age of forty-four after living his entire life as a farmer and finding favor with God through faith and by praying to him every day. William was kind, but he didn't accept excuses. He expected nothing less than an all-out effort from all of his angels — just what was expected of him.

"I called you here because we've had a case slip through the cracks," William said to Andrew. "It seems that we were going to give up on this one as hopeless, but we may not have to. This person has three generations of ancestors in heaven; we've had requests from his great-grandfather, his grandfather, and his father to give it one more try. I need you to assign someone to this right away, and it's not going to be easy, so put a good angel on this one."

"How far gone is he?" Andrew asked.

"He's almost locked in for the other side," William said. "I need you to review his life and do the best you can. I hope you can bring him back. If you can't, it could affect his two children and his ex-wife. We could lose them all. You know once the other side gets a man's soul, it affects how his children are raised. Then, in turn, it takes an extraordinary person to break the pattern in future generations."

"I know, sir," Andrew said. "I'll do the best I can. By the way, have you heard anything about me from the top?"

"Now, you know I have very little control over things like that," William said. "Although I'm sure this case would count for a lot, if you brought him back."

Andrew went back to his sector and told Phillip about his predicament, explaining about the special request from the man's relatives, and how important this was to all of heaven. They were willing to give it one more chance with an all-out fight.

Andrew asked, "Who do we have that we can put on this one?"

"We only have one angel left," Phillip said. "Everyone else is out on assignment."

"Who is it?" Andrew asked.

"Alexander Hargrove."

"No! There must be someone else."

"I'm sorry, sir. He's the only one we have at the moment."

"Pull someone back, then," said Andrew.

"You know we can't do that," Phillip said. "If we do, we'd be giving up a soul we most likely will get in favor of a soul that we aren't sure we can secure. It wouldn't be wise. Besides, you've passed him over the last two times. If you pass him over again, it won't look good for him, or for you."

Andrew sighed and said, "Bring him to me."

When he was on earth, Alexander Hargrove was a plump little man with warm, calm eyes. He had been a factory worker, and died at the age of twenty-nine during the influenza outbreak in the early 1900s. Alexander had been a good family man and a hard worker his entire life, never forgetting to thank God daily for his blessings. However, he had never been seen as highly intelligent and he got into some trouble with gambling and women before straightening himself out.

He promptly appeared before Andrew, who said, "Mr. Hargrove, I have an assignment for you."

"For me, sir, are you sure?"

"Yes, I'm sure," Andrew replied. "I have a lost soul named Timothy Fletcher that I need you to retrieve. He would be a fourth-generation entry if we can secure him, and it will have an impact for years to come if we don't. He has two children also who could be lost if you're unsuccessful. You know how we hate to let the other side get its grip on ones so young. It makes it ten times as hard to save them after they become adults."

"Are you sure you don't want to give it to someone with more experience?" Alexander asked. "I haven't been on an assignment in such a long time."

"No," Andrew replied. "You're the only one we have available right now. Let's review Timothy's life and then you'll be dispatched back to earth immediately. I have Timothy's life records right up through the present, so you'll know everything about him. Watch carefully so you can come up with a plan to bring him back to us."

Andrew waved his hand at what looked like a large television screen. It flickered to life, showing a chubby baby lying in a hospital crib.

"Timothy Fletcher was born in 1976," Andrew said. "Here he is shortly after his birth. Now let's see his father and mother."

"Oh, Roberta, he's wonderful," Timothy's father, Gerald, said. "We'll name him Timothy after my father. He'll grow to be compassionate like you and hard working like me. Thank you, God. I will thank you every day for the rest of my life for giving me such a wonderful son."

The two happy parents took Timothy home to their small town in Wisconsin, the dairy capital of America. The area had been good to Gerald's family at times and not so good at others. For three generations, they had made a living dairy farming and had done everything they could to keep the farm in the family.

When Timothy was just over a year old, he was very ill — almost on his deathbed. Dr. Cambridge, their family physician for years, came over and examined him, telling his father, "Gerald, this is influenza. You know we've lost six people in the area in the last two weeks from it. Roberta is down with it too and, being pregnant, she needs her rest. You must keep cold compresses on his forehead to help keep him cool. He may be up much of the night needing you to comfort him. Give him children's Tylenol twice a day to help break the fever. At his age our biggest concern is that he'll become dehydrated. If he doesn't take liquids for more than twelve hours or if his condition worsens and his fever increases, call me, and I'll meet you at the hospital. Can you handle it?"

Gerald's stomach was in knots. He took a deep breath, swallowed hard and said with a determined expression, "I love Timothy and I'll stay up ten nights if I have to. I'll do what has to be done."

Gerald stayed awake the entire night nursing his son and wife back to health. He applied cold compresses to Timothy's body every hour to try to break the fever, just as

Dr. Cambridge said, while his wife rested. He almost never left his son's side.

Timothy's fever worsened. Gerald felt helpless, as if he couldn't go on. He took one last deep breath and dug deep inside himself using his faith as encouragement. He prayed to God for help, saying, "God, I know I'm an ordinary man of no real significance. Could you please help my son get though this crisis and restore his health? I ask this favor of you, knowing that you have full power to do so. I believe in you fully, and I'm putting his life in your hands. Please, God. Help my son."

"I like his father," Alexander said.

"Yes, I do too," Andrew said. "And he is with us now."

Andrew and Alexander continued to watch scenes from Timothy's life. They saw Timothy slowly recover from the flu because of his father's constant care, along with a little help from above. In two weeks' time, Timothy was doing much better, and so was his mother, Roberta.

In the process, two of Gerald's cows became ill because they needed constant attention and Gerald wasn't there to give it to them. One of the cows died, causing a financial strain because every penny counted in those days.

Gerald went out into the barn and felt terrible knowing he had neglected his livestock. His stomach turned when he realized how difficult it would be to overcome the loss. He looked up with great faith and in an instant was filled with great hope from above. He prayed, "Thank you God for saving my son's life. I know you watched over him because I felt your presence the entire time he was ill. I know you will help us overcome the financial loss we have incurred as you always do. Please watch over Roberta and Timothy.

Help me stay strong and accept your will without question."

"He seems to have had the right philosophy," Alexander said as the action paused. "He had so much adversity for one person to bear, but never questioned it one bit."

"There's much more," Andrew said.

"So was he healthy after that?" Alexander asked.

"Timothy made a full recovery. And as always, time passed quickly and things like Gerald's nursing Timothy back to health were forgotten — except by us, of course. You know we remember everything, good or bad, about a man's life.

"The farm had been in Gerald's family for three generations, with each successive generation teaching the next one the value of hard work. It actually provided a decent living for Gerald a good part of the time. You would think that, if a farm had been in your family for so many years, it would be paid off, but that wasn't the case. If crops were bad and milk prices dropped, they would have to go to the bank and beg for money and another mortgage would go on the property. When the farm did well, those years were spent trying to pay down what they owed. It was a grueling cycle for many farm families."

"Couldn't they save enough money to at least give them a cushion?" Alexander asked.

"They tried to supplement their income by growing corn, for their own cattle feed and to sell," Andrew said. "It helped, but it was never enough; something would always prevent them from getting too far ahead and becoming complacent. But Gerald always managed to barely hang on, as if he was invincible. We were there watching over him to make sure it didn't get out of hand. So much hardship came their way, but you know that hardship builds good moral character."

Hearing these words, Alexander felt comforted that he was amongst others who were worthy emissaries of God instead of with the other side. He gazed with new appreciation at the two humble mortals on the screen: Gerald was a stern man with a relentless work ethic, who knew his farm inside and out, and Roberta was a kind-hearted woman that any man would be proud to call his wife.

Timothy's life began to play again. Almost two years to the day after Timothy was born, Roberta gave birth to a healthy son, whom they named Markus. A year and a half later, Roberta gave birth to a baby girl. They named her Cynthia after Gerald's grandmother. However, the birth was a difficult one and resulted in Roberta's not being able to bear any more children.

"They seem like such good parents," Alexander said. "Why were they not able to have more children?"

"They were good parents," Andrew agreed. "But we're not in any position to question why things like that happen. We must have faith that there is a good reason.

"By the time each of the boys reached the age of two, they were encouraged to do the simplest things to help out, like throwing grain to the chickens or letting their father know if the animals didn't have enough water. By the time Timothy was five, he had a regular routine where he would get up in the morning and go help his father do whatever needed to be done. Gerald believed that you had to instill a positive work ethic in children at a very young age and then they would follow your lead and never stray."

Andrew froze Timothy's life again and Alexander said, "Gerald was indeed a good man. I respect how he wanted to teach Timothy to eventually take over the farm."

"You're right," Andrew concurred. "He was a good man, but you know about free will and how things sometimes don't turn out how they should. God gives man free will to choose his own path. It's man that ultimately creates his own destiny."

"I know," Alexander agreed. "Free will is a gift to mankind, a gift that many times can tempt men and lead them astray."

Andrew started the life review again, now showing Timothy at seven years old. Timothy came inside from where he was helping in the fields to go to the bathroom. His mother and sister were at the grocery store. Roberta had baked a strawberry pie that morning and left it sitting on the counter. It was between lunch and dinner and Timothy was very hungry. After he used the bathroom, he realized just how hungry he was and let temptation get the best of him. He picked up the pie and took the whole thing outside, behind the barn. He began to eat it until there was about half left. He couldn't eat any more, so he pitched the rest in a drainage ditch out by the road. He figured that his mother would just think someone else took it. He went back to the field where his brother and father were working and acted as if nothing had happened.

When his mother came back from the store, she immediately noticed the pie was missing. After everyone came inside, she asked, "Gerald, did you see what happened to my strawberry pie? I left it on the counter and it's gone."

Gerald looked puzzled. "No, I didn't see it." He turned to Timothy. "Did you take it?"

Timothy looked away, hesitated a little and said, "No. I haven't seen it." Timothy's stomach did a flip-flop and he felt empty inside.

His dad, being a just man, wanted to believe his son, but he had a suspicion Timothy was lying. "Do you want to think about that answer, son? You were the only one in the house; Markus was outside with me the entire time."

"No, Daddy," Timothy said. "I didn't take it." Guilt-ridden, Timothy wanted to cry, but held back in fear of getting in trouble.

"Oh, Andrew," Alexander said. "You know how lies just pile up on one another and eventually you get caught. He should've owned up to it."

"I know," Andrew said. "Just watch."

Gerald wanted to make his son ponder what he had done and figured guilt would eventually win out. At dinner-time, Timothy could barely touch his meal and it became painfully obvious that he had indeed taken the pie. After dinner, Gerald said, "I find it a little odd that you barely touched your meal after a long day of work. Are you sure you didn't take the pie, Timmy?"

"Oh no, Father, not me," Timothy said. Timothy's face was stricken with guilt. Roberta frowned and looked concerned as Timothy slouched a little in his chair and then looked away.

Later that evening, just before sunset, Gerald went outside to feed his cows and make sure they had enough water for the night. He saw a large gathering of birds out by the drainage ditch, and went to see what all the fuss was about. Sure enough, Gerald found the pie plate with a few scraps from the filling left on it. The rest of the pie had been eaten by the birds. He grabbed the plate and took it inside and called for Timothy.

After Timothy came Gerald asked, "Are you sure there's nothing you want to tell me?"

Timothy nervously rubbed his palms and said "No, father."

Gerald pulled out the pie plate and said, "I found this in the ditch by the road – the ditch where I think you threw it." He stared his son down.

Timothy, rubbing his hands on the side of his hips, looked down at the ground and broke down and cried, "Yes, Father, I took the pie today. I was hungry and couldn't help it."

Disappointed, Gerald said, "You must never tell a lie, because it will turn a bad situation into something much worse. A lie always does. I'll be back in a little while to give you your punishment, after I discuss this with your mother."

He left Timothy to worry for a bit and came back about ten minutes later. He said, "Son, I have no choice but to give you five whacks with my belt. I don't want to, but you must learn how to tell right from wrong."

Gerald caught hold of Timothy, put him over his knee, and smacked him five times with his belt. Being sympathetic, he left Timothy's pants up so the blows wouldn't be as painful. In fact, they didn't even leave a mark.

Timothy, more frightened than anything, screamed with each strike.

When Gerald was finished he said, "I love you son, but you must learn to never tell lies."

Timothy's face turned beet-red and he was filled with rage. It was a sad day for them both, with two significant results: Gerald resolved never to hit Timothy again, and Timothy had his first feelings of resentment toward his father.

"I don't like where this is going," Alexander said, as Andrew paused the action.

"You have no idea just how hard this assignment is going to be," Andrew said. "But time has a way of healing almost everything, as we will see."

Alexander gulped and thought, *I hope I can come through this time! If I don't, they might not give me another assignment for a long time.*

❧ 2 ❧

Timothy's life began playing again for the angels to view. Markus followed in his brother's footsteps and did the things Timothy used to do when he was his age. Gerald was pleased that his sons were progressing well and that he would have not one, but two strong heirs who could one day take over the farm.

"Now watch this episode when Markus was six and Timothy was eight," Andrew said.

"Markus, make sure you feed the chickens enough," Timothy told his brother.

"I always do," Markus replied; then he started coughing and bent over. Timothy glanced at his brother and didn't think anything of it at first. Markus continued to cough and soon couldn't breathe. He started to wheeze almost as if he was choking. Timothy's face turned white as he was gripped by fear. He rushed over to his father and said, "There's something wrong with Markus!"

Gerald's heart raced, and with a look of dire concern he rushed over to his younger son. Markus was now on the ground, gasping for air. Gerald asked, "What's wrong, son? Can you speak?" When Markus just continued gasping, Gerald scooped him up and rushed him off to the hospital.

The family spent three seemingly endless hours in the emergency waiting room, wondering if Markus was going to be all right. When the doctor came into the waiting area, he said, "Markus is doing much better, but he has a very bad case of asthma. It's always a matter for concern when a child is diagnosed at such an early age. We need to come up with an ongoing treatment plan. These cases can be controlled with inhalers and medication, and on rare occasions, some children do outgrow the condition. Only time will tell." Gerald and Roberta were upset, but thankful that their son was all right.

"Now watch carefully, Alexander," Andrew said. "This is where Gerald caught our eye and made us realize he was probably going to be one of us."

Gerald went home and prayed that night, "God, I am thankful Markus is alive and doing well. If it is your will for my son to have a lifelong medical condition, then so be it. I have complete faith in your judgment and I'm turning myself over to you. Please guide me in what to do next. Please help me."

"Do you see how he put his faith first, instead of being bitter and blaming anyone?" Andrew said. "That's what I call a real man. Now watch."

When Markus had his follow-up appointment a few days later, the doctor said, "Markus has a chronic case of asthma. He may be having a normal day and then suddenly have an attack. He must carry an inhaler with him at all times. He will also have to take medication on a daily basis to reduce the chances of an attack. I'll write the prescriptions and I'd like to see him back in a month."

"What about sports?" Gerald asked. "Everyone in my family has always played baseball and I want Markus to as well."

"Let's see how he responds to the medication," the doctor said. "Many people with asthma live normal lives while others must restrict their activities. At this point, we can't predict the severity of his symptoms."

That night, after Gerald and Roberta had put the kids to bed, Gerald emotionally said, "I don't know how we're going to be able to afford the medication for Markus if he has to take it for an extended period of time. You know we're in the middle of a terrible drought and we could lose half our crop. Feed prices have increased and milk prices haven't caught up yet."

Roberta rested her hand gently on his arm and said, "You need to stop being so negative. Where's your faith? You know there's a purpose for everything. I believe everything will work out and Markus will be fine. Shouldn't you?"

"You're right, of course," Gerald said. "I'll put his destiny and mine in the hands of God." That night, he prayed for help with all his strength, heart, mind, body, and soul. "God, strengthen me to be a good man. Help me to follow you and not to resent your will. I need you to direct me down the right path. I am a simple man and need help. I believe you will show me the way."

"Again, this caught our attention," Andrew said. "Gerald was shown favor from above. It rained the next day and most of his crop was saved."

The two angels watched as Markus had to go back to the hospital three more times that summer, which put a great financial strain on the family. They were still struggling after that, but their situation was not as bad as it could have been. Somehow Gerald found the money every month for Markus' prescriptions.

"So what happened to Markus?" Alexander asked. "Was he all right after that? Did he get to play baseball?"

"Just watch," Andrew said.

Gerald had always made sure both Timothy and Markus had their own baseball gloves, and tried to practice with them every day after all the work was done. He set up a target on a tree and Timothy practiced pitching. When he was eight, Timothy joined his first team. He was the best pitcher in the league that year and became a great hitter as well.

Markus also joined the same team once he turned eight, but didn't like it very much, in part because of his illness. He never had the drive and motivation Timothy did, so he rarely practiced. He continued to play, but only to appease his father.

Now the angels saw Timothy and Markus at a baseball game later that season. The score was three to two and their team was winning. In the last inning, their team needed one more out to win the game to seal a playoff spot. The other team had runners on second and third base. An easy pop fly was hit to Markus in right field. He got under the fly ball and misjudged it. The ball fell to the ground and two runs were scored. They lost the game and the chance to go to the playoffs.

Afterward, one of Timothy's friends on the team said, "Your brother stinks. He shouldn't even be playing baseball."

Another boy said, "He cost us a playoff spot. He's the worst player on the team."

"Instead of sticking up for his brother he was tempted by the other side," Andrew said. "He could've really made a difference in his brother's life with a few encouraging words."

Timothy said, "Yeah he really does stink. I wish he wasn't even on our team." Markus walked by and Timothy tried to save face with his friends by saying, "You couldn't even catch that easy pop fly. What's wrong with you? Can't you do anything right?"

Markus' distress was apparent when his shoulders drooped and he threw his glove down. He said, "I tried the best I could. I hate baseball and I hate you." Markus ran to the car while all the other kids laughed. The coach walked up and sternly said, "Break it up! Every one of you is going to run five laps around the bases for showing poor sportsmanship. Now get moving!"

On the way home, Timothy didn't say a word to Markus.

When Timothy was ten, he began to feel more resentment toward his brother and sister. One hot summer day, he was helping his father in the vegetable garden when he asked, "Dad, why does Markus always get out of most of the work? I know he has asthma, but you've always told me that hard work is good for a boy."

Gerald replied, "The doctor told me that in the summertime his asthma can be triggered much easier than in the winter. I don't like to take chances with him. He still does chores."

"He gets all the easy jobs while I have to do the hard ones," Timothy said. "It's not fair!"

"You're much older and stronger than he is," Gerald replied. "You've been given one of the greatest gifts there is: your health. You should always be thankful for what you have and not worry about what other people have or do. My father taught me that."

"But Dad," Timothy said, "what about Cindy? Why doesn't she have to work the fields like I do?"

"She's a girl," Gerald said. "She's only six, and she helps your mother with all of the chores in the house. You don't expect your mother to do all the cooking, laundry, and cleaning all by herself?"

"Well, no," Timothy said. "It seems like they have it so easy and I don't."

Gerald sat down on a nearby bench and said, "Sit down." Timothy sat down next to his father. Gerald continued, "I know it seems like you're always working, but we have to do these things to survive. When I was your age, I did the same. At the time I didn't like all the hard work either, but now I'm glad I did it. We have our own land, and I'm thankful we've held on to it as long as we have. Son, you always need to be grateful, no matter what. I can't emphasize that enough. Listen, why don't you and I throw the ball around after dinner? I know you have a game Friday and you could use the practice."

With a huge smile on his face, Timothy said, "All right, Dad. I can't wait."

Later that afternoon, Gerald came in for dinner and grumbled, "It always seems like something holds us back. The tractor broke down again and I have to get it fixed. It seems like the work never stops around here."

"I won't have any of that complaining," Roberta said. "You're setting a bad example for the children. You'll get your tractor fixed tonight and everything will be back to normal tomorrow. Then all that complaining will be for nothing."

Gerald sat down and Cindy walked into the room. She went over to her father and jumped on his lap. She said, "Daddy, I missed you so much today. Will you read me a story, please, please?"

Gerald hugged and kissed Cindy and said, "Sure, go pick out a book and we'll sit together on the couch."

Cindy went and picked out a book, brought it back, and said, "I love you, Daddy."

Gerald's heart melted and he said, "I love you too, Pumpkin." With Markus on one side and Cindy on the other, he read them a story. He always put his own twist on the stories he read and changed the ending so that no matter how many times he read them, they were never the same. They laughed and had a great time while, unnoticed, Timothy went outside and picked up his baseball glove. He threw the ball around by himself for a while, figuring that he would have his time with his father after dinner, as Gerald had promised.

"Let me guess," Alexander said. "Gerald never got to play with Timothy that day."

"You keep interrupting," Andrew said. "Just watch."

After dinner, Gerald went outside and started working on the tractor. After about an hour of waiting and fidgeting, Timothy approached him. "Dad, I'm ready to play catch."

Gerald looked up, frustrated, and said, "I can't get this carburetor to work right. I've cleaned it as best as I can and the engine still won't start. I'm going to have to take it apart and go get some parts first thing in the morning. This tractor has to be running by tomorrow. We need to get the crops planted."

"Are you going to have time to throw the ball with me after you're done?" Timothy asked.

"I don't know, son," Gerald responded. "This carburetor is giving me fits. Hand me that half-inch wrench, will you?"

Timothy handed him the wrench and said, "If you can come over and play catch, I'll be over at the tree where I practice. I love you, Dad."

"I love you too," Gerald said. Then he groaned in frustration at the tractor.

Timothy went over to the tree and kicked it hard. He practiced his slider for an hour, angrily, and then went inside after that. Gerald worked on the tractor until almost dark and was absolutely exhausted when he was through. He never did play with his son that day.

"Oh Andrew," Alexander said. "He could've gone over and played for a little while. He should've made the effort."

"I never said Gerald was perfect," said Andrew. "I just said he was one of us. Now we're up to when Timothy was eleven."

Timothy was in the next room listening when Gerald walked in one afternoon and said, "Roberta, I'm worried. This time we might lose the farm. You know how dairy prices have dropped thirty percent, and the corn crop isn't that strong this year. Then there's those two calves we lost at birth. The vet bills are huge and I don't know what to do. It seems like our luck is never going to change. I'm going to go to the bank tomorrow and ask for a personal loan. If they won't give it to me, I'm going to ask if they'll refinance our mortgage. I hope they'll go for it."

Roberta took it in stride, as usual, and said, "Have faith. Have you learned nothing your whole life? This farm has been in your family for eighty years, and things will work out somehow. You'll see."

Gerald frowned, then wrapped his arms around her. "I don't know what I'd do without you. You're the best wife in the world. Thank you for always being there when I need you."

"When I took a vow to be your wife, I promised to love you in good times and bad. I'll keep that promise as long as I live."

Gerald kissed her and said, "I love you, dear."

Timothy felt sad for his father at first. He knew how hard he worked every day. But then he was tempted with contradictory thoughts: *Why should I worry about the farm? We would probably be better off without it. All we do is work all day and we can't even make enough money to pay our bills. If Dad had a real job like some of my friends' fathers, we could have nice things like they do.*

Andrew interrupted, "I wish we had sent someone into Timothy's life at that point. It would've been much easier to sway him our way. I guess we thought since Gerald was such a good man that things would work out."

Roberta prayed long and hard that night for help to keep her family safe. She was very careful not to ask for money specifically; she just asked for her family to be watched over and taken care of.

Sure enough, sixty days later the mortgage was approved and they were able to keep the farm. The day his father went to sign the papers, Timothy was riddled with more doubt. He thought, *I don't know if I want to live like this the rest of my life. Father is a good man but he struggles so much. How can he enjoy life always worrying about losing the farm? There has to be more to life than just surviving. I don't think I want to be a farmer when I grow up. I want to go out and see the world and be free.*

The onscreen images froze. "Wouldn't Gerald know by now that things were going to work out?" Alexander asked. "His faith is great and he has a terrific wife who has great faith as well. He knows the farm inside and out, and he's quite good at running it."

"You know how men are," Andrew said. "They're providers and look at supporting their families as their number one job in life. Every good man worries at times about money and being a good father. Gerald was no different."

After the mortgage was approved, the farm thrived for a few years. When Timothy was fourteen, something happened that pushed him in the wrong direction. Baseball had become Timothy's escape from all his frustrations in life. Markus had quit baseball after two seasons, which made

Timothy want to excel at it even more. Gerald had accepted that Markus' illness would prevent him from ever playing again.

Timothy practiced his pitching, day in and day out, and became one of the best pitchers in his league. At the end of the season, his team made the playoffs and was in the finals for the league championship.

Gerald had worked all day as usual, but he gave Timothy the day off so he would be well rested for the evening game. Roberta took him to the field early for practice and to warm up. Gerald was going to bring Cindy and Markus a little later, after his work was done.

Markus was getting ready to go when he started gasping for air. Gerald ran up to him and asked, "Are you all right?" Markus continued gasping until Gerald finally put him and Cindy in the car and rushed them to the hospital. He got a message to Roberta that he had done so, and she made arrangements for one of the other parents to drive Timothy home, but didn't tell him about the emergency for fear that it would affect his performance. She left in the first inning before she even got a chance to see Timothy pitch.

Timothy noticed that his dad and mom weren't at the game and wondered why. His anger overcame him and it was almost as if he was possessed. He was unstoppable, pitching a two-hitter and winning the championship for his team.

After the last out, his team members swarmed him and congratulated him. One boy said, "You're a great pitcher! That was one of the best games I've ever seen!" Another said, "We won! I can't believe it! You were incredible."

Coach Jeff Paddington came up to Timothy and said, "Good game, Tim! That slider you brought today was wicked. I want you to know that that was one of the best performances any player I've ever coached has had. You keep it up and you have a real chance to make it as a pro."

All the acclaim Timothy received couldn't make up for the fact that not one family member had been there to witness what was surely his best game ever. He felt let down, discouraged, and frustrated. He thought, *Why didn't Dad come and see the game? Why did Mom leave? I'll bet it was something to do with the farm.*

Timothy went home to an empty house. No one had even left him a note. Timothy was worried at first but then figured it was probably something to do with Markus. He became irate, and even though his arm was a little sore, he went outside and threw the baseball harder and with more determination than ever.

When the family returned, Gerald found Timothy lying on his bed in his room. He sat down, looked at Timothy, and said, "I'm sorry about the game, son. Markus had a terrible attack and I had to take him to the hospital. I was so worried, but he's going to be all right. How did you do?"

All Timothy's anger boiled to the surface. "I figured it was Markus again! That was the championship game! You missed it. I pitched a two-hitter and we won three to nothing."

"Don't you dare use that tone with me! Your brother was sick and needed help."

"Markus is always sick!" Timothy cried. "You never cared about me like you do about Cindy and Markus. I wish you weren't my father."

Gerald, overworked and frustrated, grabbed Timothy by the shirt. "How dare you talk to me like that! I didn't raise you to be so ungrateful. Show some respect for all we've done for you. If I had talked to my father like that, he would've knocked me out."

Roberta hurried into the room. "Gerald, don't! Let go of that boy right now!"

Gerald realized he shouldn't have lost his temper and felt ashamed. He released his son's shirt and said, "I'm sorry."

Timothy glared at his father and cried, "I hate you!" He got up and left the room.

Gerald was left sitting there, hurt and not knowing what to do. Roberta hugged him and said, "Give him some time. He'll cool off and then you can talk to him."

"Have I failed as a father?"

"No, dear, you're a great father," Roberta said, "Boys are very self-centered at Timothy's age and that game was one of the most important things in his life. I think if you talk to Tim in the morning, once his temper has settled down, everything will be fine."

"I hope you're right," Gerald said. "I feel like Tim is pulling away from me and, no matter what I do, it's not good enough."

"You have to give him a little time to realize you were right. None of us has control over when Markus has an attack, and of course you had to take him to the hospital, no matter what else was going on at the time."

"I feel like I can't talk to him anymore," Gerald said. "He's so stubborn these days."

"Sort of like you when you were his age," Roberta replied with a smile.

"Maybe you're right, dear. I'll talk to him tomorrow."

The next morning, Gerald approached Timothy and said, "Son, I'm sorry I didn't make it to your game yesterday, but you must understand that your brother's health was in jeopardy. I would do the same for you if you were ill."

Timothy, still stewing, said, "It's all right. Can we just get to work?" Then he walked out to the milking barn.

Gerald's feelings softened. He wanted so desperately to reach out to his son and help him see how much he loved him. He said a quick prayer. *God, please help Timothy understand that I love him and only want the best for all my children. He's at a difficult age and needs your help. Come to him and help him find his way.*

He felt a lot better after that. He decided to let Timothy cool off a little more and went about his work for the day. Meanwhile, Timothy held his frustration in, and turned away even more from his father.

Timothy practiced baseball every chance he could after that. It became an obsession. When it came time to go to high school, he tried out and made the varsity team as a freshman. He became accustomed to the acclaim that being a star pitcher brought. Baseball was his way to show the world that he was someone special and that he had extraordinary talent. His relationship with his father deteriorated more along the way, with them butting heads about chores and just about everything else. But during all that time, Gerald never lost faith, and he prayed for his son daily.

When Timothy was a junior in high school, his team's practices grew longer and harder. His coach realized that they had a great team, and pushed the players more than ever before. This affected Timothy's ability to help his father with the work on the farm. One day when Timothy was sixteen, Gerald told him, "I need your help with the planting tomorrow. We have to get these crops in before it's too late."

"I can't," Timothy said. "I have a huge game coming up and our practices are doubled for the next two days."

"I'm depending on you, son," Gerald said. "We're all depending on you."

"I can't!" Timothy repeated. "We have a shot at the state championship and Coach Emery said practices are mandatory."

Gerald had little patience with his son by now. He said, "Well, how about I pull you off the team? I don't have to let you play baseball. You have responsibilities here."

With Timothy's hormones raging and his built-up resentment festering, he yelled, "I'm sure you'd love to do that because all you care about is this farm! I don't ever want to be a farmer and I plan to move away as soon as I can!"

Gerald was floored, thinking, *This farm has been my family's pride and joy for years and my son is so ungrateful that he wants to move away! How can he be so hard-headed? I'll teach him.*

"You're off the team, as of right now," Gerald said. "Now go get your work clothes on."

Timothy shouted, "I hate you! I wish I could leave right now!" and he ran to his room.

"Oh no," Alexander said. "He shouldn't have told Gerald he hated him."

"I know," Andrew said. "The other side had their sights on him and I blame us a little for not fighting hard enough. He was at the most difficult part in his life and we overlooked him a bit. We should've sent a friend to help him or something, but we didn't. Now watch."

After Roberta found out what had happened, she came to Gerald in the barn and told him, "You have to apologize to Tim and let him play on the team. Baseball is his whole life right now and you're being too hard on him. I'll help you with the planting and so will Cindy. Markus will do what he can, too. We'll get the crop in, don't worry. But you have to set things right with Timothy."

"Too hard on him?" said Gerald. "He needs to become a man. He needs to work the farm."

"There's plenty of time for him to become a man," said Roberta. She touched Gerald's arm softly. "If you make him quit baseball, you'll lose him forever."

"You're right," said Gerald, "like you always are. I'll speak with him after I get done here."

After Roberta left, Gerald looked up and prayed: *I fear Timothy is pulling away from me. He's been so angry lately. Please help Timothy and me work things out. Help him see how important this farm is to our family. And give me the strength to understand what he's going through. I put my trust in you and will not question your will.*

Gerald went to Timothy's room and knocked on the closed door. After Timothy reluctantly told him to come in, Gerald said, "Son, I'm sorry about what I said. I was wrong, and I'm man enough to admit it. Get dressed for practice. Your mom will drop you off."

"But what about the planting?" Timothy asked.

"Your mother and Cindy are going to help as much as they can. Your mom reassured me that we'll get the crop in and I believe her. God has always provided for us and I'm sure he will once again. I was hoping that one day you would take over the farm just like I did from my father and he did from his father."

"I'm not sure that I want to be a farmer," Timothy said. "Maybe Markus or Cindy does."

Gerald tried to hide his horror at his son's words. He struggled to find words and finally said, "Son. I'm going to teach you something that my father taught me long ago. You shouldn't fall for the riches the world has to offer. Many men find out well after it's too late that it isn't all it's cracked up to be. Then they look back on their lives, feeling sorry, and wishing they would've done things differently. It's better to live a simple life and to find favor with God. That's why I work so hard keeping this farm. It gave my father and his father a good honest living. I put my faith in above."

"But I want more for myself than this," Timothy said. "One day I'm going to pitch in the major leagues."

"Be careful desiring something like that so much," Gerald said. "It could be your downfall. Think about what I said."

Timothy said nothing more, and went and got ready for practice.

Gerald felt as though his heart would shatter and fall to the ground. He prayed again, renewing his faith, and went back outside to continue his work, feeling a little lighter in spirit. As Timothy left, he approached his father and said, "Dad, I'm sorry too. I'll help you as much as I can when I'm done, even though these double practices are going to be tough. I know how hard you work every day and I won't let you down."

Gerald, Roberta, Markus, and Cindy were able to get the crop planted; it just took a little longer than usual. They were blessed with a bumper crop of corn that year, and the price of milk skyrocketed, too. For the first time in quite a while, the family actually had extra money after all the bills were paid.

Timothy's team went to the state championships that season, and he pitched a four-hit shutout in the finals with scouts from all over watching him. Again, he thrived on how the world couldn't seem to get enough of him when he was on the mound. His ego and desire for recognition grew more intense every time he got on the field.

Andrew paused the images onscreen and said to Alexander, "At that point in Gerald's life, he had no idea that things were about to change drastically. He and Timothy were not yet done with their differences."

❦ 3 ❦

Andrew and Alexander watched as five coaches and four recruiters came to Timothy's house during his senior year. They wanted him to pitch for their college teams, and they all offered him partial scholarships that would pay most of his way through school.

Gerald, unhappy that his oldest son questioned whether he wanted to be a farmer, wouldn't sign a commitment form to allow Timothy to go to college. Gerald used the excuse that they didn't have the money, even though the scholarships would pay for most of the tuition. He said they couldn't spare a dime for books and food, let alone pay for a dorm room, and he was telling the truth.

After Gerald refused to sign the forms he thought, *If Timothy does go away to college it's really going to hurt us badly. Maybe I should focus on Markus and Cindy more to help out just in case. I wish he would see things my way and understand how important this place is to us.*

Timothy was upset and locked himself in his room every chance he could. He felt as if he was living with strangers.

His feelings toward his father worsened with each passing day, until about a week before an important signing deadline. A recruiter from the University of Wisconsin came to see Gerald. His name was John Salazar and he'd been to the farm before. This time he brought someone else with him.

Gerald invited the two men inside. The man he didn't know said, "My name is Brian Tate. I'm the athletic director from the University of Wisconsin. Is Tim here?"

Gerald said, "Yes, I'll go get him." He came back with Timothy while Cindy, Markus, and Roberta all followed.

Everyone sat down. Brian Tate said, "Timothy, Mr. Fletcher, I'm willing to offer your son a full scholarship to the University of Wisconsin. This will include tuition, books, food, and lodging. Everything will be paid for. In turn, Timothy will have to agree to play baseball for us for at least three years. As you know, we aren't allowed to offer him any type of monetary compensation."

Gerald took a deep breath and said, "We'll think about it and let you know after I discuss it with my wife and son in private. You can contact us tomorrow for the answer."

"Dad!" Timothy said. "Tell him we'll take it right now, please dad, tell him."

"We'll discuss it in private and get back with him," Gerald said. "We have a lot of things to consider."

"What?" Timothy asked. "The farm?"

Roberta, seeing that a huge argument was in the making, said, "Timothy! Don't you dare question your father! He said that we'll discuss it and we will, tonight."

"I just don't understand why you can't tell him yes now," argued Timothy.

"Because dad needs you here," Markus said. 'How will he ever get by without you?"

"Well I guess you'll just have to do more, won't you?" Timothy snidely returned.

"Yeah, well at least I treat mom and dad with respect," Markus said.

Timothy stood up, made a fist and was just about to say something else to Markus when Roberta spoke up. "Now that's enough. I don't want to hear another word from either of you and I mean it!"

Roberta glanced at John and Brian, who had blank looks on their faces, and said, "We'll get back to you in a day or so, if that's all right?"

"That will be fine," Brian said. "Remember the signing deadline is in five days. We must know before then. Oh, one other thing. We are expecting to have a great team. Many pro scouts will be looking at all our players. This is a great opportunity."

Timothy's eyes lit up at that. Brian continued, "Thanks, and we hope to hear from you either way."

Leaving it at that, Brian and John left.

"Did he take the scholarship?" Alexander asked.

"You'll see," replied Andrew.

That night, Gerald sat down with Roberta and said, "Honey, I don't know what to do. I want Timothy to be able to go to college, but I need him here too. What do you think we should do?"

Roberta looked at Gerald with calming eyes and said, "The boy's heart is in baseball right now. You must let him go. If you don't, he will always resent the fact that you took his chance to play college baseball away from you. We'll get by, just as we always have, and Tim will be back after he grows up a little."

Gerald listened to his wife and signed the commitment form the next day. When it came time, Timothy packed his things and got ready to leave for college. On the day he left, Markus, Cindy, Gerald and Roberta all went to see him off. Roberta had tears in her eyes and Gerald was equally sad.

Timothy said, "I'm going to miss you all very much. It's not like I won't be home when school isn't in. Please don't cry, mom."

Everyone hugged Timothy, Roberta last of all. As he embraced his mother he said, "I'll be back as much as I can. Everything will be fine."

Timothy got on the bus for Madison and his family stood and watched it pull away. He was very sad at first, but on the other hand, he was anxious to get his life started as an adult and was glad to be on his own. He felt like he had given his entire life to helping other people and now wanted to focus on himself.

"Oh no," Alexander said. "I know what happens to people when they only think of themselves. They usually self-destruct. I'm afraid to watch what happens next."

"Indeed. Timothy has some hard lessons to learn," Andrew replied.

❦

Timothy was nervous before his first college game, but when he stepped on the mound everything changed. He pitched a five-hit, one-run game and had his first victory. He soon became comfortable on the field and was an instant favorite with the crowd and his teammates. People cheered every time he struck someone out, which boosted the rest of the team's performance. His grades were good and he even met a girl named Carrie and dated her for a few months.

Timothy's family could only afford to come to two games all season which didn't seem to bother him much. The rush of being in the limelight superseded almost everything. Timothy's mind was focused on one thing only: becoming a professional baseball player. He pitched well the rest of his first year at college, winning fourteen games and losing six.

Back home, Gerald and Roberta managed the farm as best they could. They hired a part-time worker, which was all they could afford, but it wasn't enough. The crops suffered from drought and they got behind on their bills. On top of everything else, they lost two calves at birth.

Markus didn't plan to go to college because his grades weren't very good and they didn't have the money anyway. Instead, he wanted to help his father as much as he could. After school and on weekends, Markus learned everything about the farm inside and out. He loved his father dearly and felt that he would have to be the one who took over the farm. He knew Timothy didn't have the desire to come back even though Gerald refused to give up hope and was in denial.

The stress on everyone finally took its toll when Markus was out helping milk the cows. He started breathing heavily; Gerald rushed over to him and asked, "Are you all right?"

Markus gasped for air and shook his head.

Gerald rushed him to the hospital and waited with Roberta and Cindy in the emergency room for two hours.

When Dr. Richter came out he said, "Markus will be all right. He had another attack. Has he been under a lot of stress lately?"

"We've all been under a lot of stress," Roberta said.

"Try to limit the stress for a while, and let him get some rest and he should be fine. He can go home as soon as he's ready. You can see him now if you'd like."

When Gerald, Roberta and Cindy went in to see Markus he said, "I'm sorry, Father. I know how things are for us now. If I were healthier things would be different."

"Don't you ever believe for one moment that I wouldn't give up everything I had for any of my children in a moment's notice," Gerald said. "I love you and I'm just happy you're all right."

"I love you too, Dad," Markus said.

"When Timothy gets back from school everything will be better," Gerald said.

"We'll get through whatever we have to," Roberta added. They all hugged tightly and then Markus got dressed and they all went home.

Alexander looked at Andrew sadly and said, "These are good people."

"Yes they are," Andrew agreed. "Now you know why we have to send you back. Keep watching."

At the end of his freshman year, Timothy came home and helped out on the farm, although grudgingly. Nothing could satisfy him like the cheers from the crowd when he was on the baseball field, and he detested farm work more than ever.

Gerald worried that Timothy had become engrossed with all the world had to offer, and that he would give in to the strong temptations that he would inevitably face in the near future. Timothy was more distant than ever from Gerald and could barely hold a conversation with his father without it turning into an argument.

A few days before Timothy was to go back to school for his sophomore year, Roberta approached Gerald while he was cleaning one of the milking machines in the barn and said, "Tim has changed so much. I feel he's even more distant from me."

"I feel like I've failed as a father," Gerald said. "Not only has he turned away from us, I fear he has turned away from God."

"You haven't failed, dear," Roberta said. "You're the best father I've ever seen. I'm going to try to talk to him. Maybe if I tell him how we feel he might realize how much we love him."

Roberta approached Timothy when he was up in his room listening to music and said, "I'd like to have a talk with you."

"What is it?" Timothy asked.

"I've seen a change in you since you went to college," Roberta said. "Is everything all right?"

"Everything is fine," Timothy said. "I'm doing great in school and I'm pitching better than ever."

"No, I mean is everything all right with you inside? You seem so different. You're focused on worldly things so much. You never go to church with us on Sunday anymore."

"If being a college ball player is worldly, then I guess I'm guilty," Timothy said. "I'm not ten years old anymore,

Mom. I'm a man and I know what I'm doing. As far as church, I sat through it every Sunday for years. I remember everything they said."

"Bite your tongue, Timothy Fletcher!" Roberta said. "I'm just worried that—"

Timothy cut her off. "Don't worry about me. I can take care of myself." Then he walked out of the room. Roberta's eyes filled with tears; Timothy was more distant than she had thought.

Timothy built a respectable record over the next two baseball seasons. With each passing game he became more accustomed to people cheering for him and he relished the rush he got every time he stepped on the mound. He won fifteen games and lost six in his sophomore year; in his junior year, his record was sixteen and four with one more game to go. Scouts came from many of the major league teams to watch Timothy pitch that day, hoping they would be the one to sign him.

During the last game of his junior year, Timothy was on the mound in the sixth inning of a scoreless game. He reared back to throw a slider, but when he released it, he fell to the ground in pain. His trainer ran out to him and asked, "What's wrong?"

Timothy managed to get up and said, "I hurt my arm bad. It feels like there's a hundred needles sticking in my elbow. I can't move my arm at all. I can't let the scouts see me like this. I need to keep pitching."

The trainer touched Timothy's arm and he winced in pain. The trainer said, "You're done for the day," and escorted Timothy off the field with all the scouts watching. The trainer took him to the hospital.

Timothy had to have an MRI on his elbow. Roberta came all the way to Madison to accompany him at the hospital. At the follow up appointment, Dr. Mackenzie, his new physician, explained, "I'm afraid you have a torn ulnar collateral ligament in your elbow, just as I suspected. Your condition is better known as the Tommy John injury."

Dr. Mackenzie walked over to an eraser board that was off to the side of the room and started drawing a picture. He said, "Think of the ligament in your elbow as a bearing or a washer that protects and separates your two joints from rubbing together. Over the years, with the repeated motion of throwing, the ligament stretches and in time gets worn out. Eventually your elbow becomes like two pieces of metal rubbing together. Do you throw a slider?'

"Yes, I do," Timothy said. "It's one of my best pitches."

"Just as I suspected," Dr. Mackenzie said. "Many times the motion of that pitch wears out the ulnar ligament more quickly.

"What I'm going to need to do is take a small piece of a ligament from your forearm and attach it into your elbow. The ligament will have to heal and take just right."

"Will I ever be able to pitch again?" Timothy asked.

"It's hard to say," Dr. Mackenzie said. "If you work really hard and the surgery goes well, you'll have a seventy-five percent chance to be as good as new by next season."

"Next season!" Timothy said. "I have to pitch next season."

"Let's not worry about that now," Dr. Mackenzie said. "Let's see how you do after surgery." After the doctor explained all the details and left the room, Timothy turned to the garbage can and kicked it. He looked at Roberta and then looked at the floor. Roberta came over to Timothy and gave him a huge hug.

Roberta felt the love for her son resonate throughout her body as she held him, the love that only a parent would feel. It had been a long time since Timothy had even been home, let alone shown any affection toward her. Timothy welcomed her embrace and responded with, "What am I going to do, Mom?"

"I'll tell you what you're going to do," Roberta said. "You're going to have that operation and work hard like the doctor said and be on that mound next year. And both of us should pray every day."

Roberta did pray every day for Timothy's recovery, and the night before the operation Timothy got on his knees and prayed too. "God, please help me fully recover, and please help me make it to the major leagues. I know I haven't been exactly a model person but please do this for me. It's all I ever wanted. Please, God, help me make it to the major leagues."

Timothy had the operation with Roberta waiting there at the hospital the entire time. Gerald was hurt that he couldn't be there, but he knew his entire family depended on him and the success of the farm. And with Timothy gone at college those three years, he just couldn't leave.

When the operation was over, Dr. Mackenzie found Roberta in the waiting room and said, "It went well. I think he's going to be just fine. I'll leave you instructions that I want Timothy to follow perfectly. In a few weeks he should be in a program to strengthen that elbow. With a little luck, he might be as good as new."

Timothy did his physical therapy program and at the end of the semester he went home, but was little help to his family. Gerald was struggling again and barely getting by. Roberta drove Timothy to physical therapy three times the first week, nearly forty miles round trip. After the first week, Markus went up to Timothy when he was sitting outside and said, "I hope you plan on giving up baseball for good now. Dad needed you over the last three years and you weren't here."

"For your information," Timothy said. "I'm going back to college next year and picking up right where I left off. I'm going to be in the major leagues. You're here for Dad. I'm sure that's all he needs."

"You know how it is," Markus said. "Running this place takes a lot of work."

"Well I never seemed to have trouble," Timothy said and then he walked away.

Cindy, standing just around the corner, had heard the entire conversation. She caught up with Timothy and said, "Don't listen to him. He's been in a bad mood lately."

"Well he doesn't need to take it out on me."

"Have you thought about what you're going to do if you can't pitch again?" Cindy asked.

"I will pitch again!" Timothy said. "I will. Now leave me alone."

"Sorry," Cindy said. And Timothy walked away.

Timothy spent the first half of the summer working hard, trying to get his arm back into shape. A few days after midsummer, Timothy was sitting out in the barn thinking when Gerald walked in and asked, "How's your arm feeling today, son?"

"It's a little better."

"Good," Gerald said. "You do know that there's a chance that you'll never get your fastball back again. I don't want to be negative, but it's something you should think about."

"You don't think I've thought about that every day since this happened?" Timothy retorted. "It's all I ever think about. I know I'll get my fastball back. I'm sure of it."

"Remember how I always told you that things happen for a reason," Gerald said.

"Yeah, I know," Timothy said uncaringly.

"I believe a man's destiny is preset," Gerald said. "I believe he can shape it a little with his choices, but ultimately he ends up where he's supposed to be. Just remember, where ever you end up is where you're supposed to be."

"I belong in the major leagues," Timothy said. "And I'll get there."

"I love you, Timothy, and if you ever need to talk, you can come to me."

"I'm fine," said Timothy, and he walked away.

After Timothy left, Gerald felt again that he had failed as a father. It was as if something inside his son was eating away at him, preventing them from being closer. He looked up and prayed, *Help Tim, God. I know he's hurting inside and he needs you. Please help him.*

Timothy spent the rest of the summer going to rehabilitation three times a week and trying to get his strength back. His hopes were fueled by the fact that he was able to throw the ball at half speed with not too much pain by the time school started again.

When school started, Timothy had five months until spring training and figured he would be in perfect condition by then. He continued his physical therapy and kept his grades up, making sure nothing would get in his way once the season started.

As training camp got underway, Timothy struggled with throwing the ball. He had pain off and on but was afraid to say anything. When he warmed up before his first exhibition game he felt nervous, but when he took the field and heard the crowd cheer, he was invigorated. A feeling of hope enveloped his body as he made his way toward the mound. When he threw his first few pitches at warm ups, he remembered how it felt to be the center of attention with thousands of people cheering him on. He remembered getting out batter after batter consistently, game after game.

The first batter came up and Timothy reared back and threw him his best pitch, his fastball. Pain shot throughout his body, starting in his elbow as he released the ball. The batter swung and drilled the ball up the gap in left field for a double. After the ball came back to the infield and it was thrown to Timothy he slammed the ball in his mitt in disgust. He threw two more pitches that were called balls by the umpire, with pain still shooting throughout Timothy's body.

He gripped the ball as tightly as he could and threw another fastball. The batter hit it deep into center field off the wall for a triple. The pain got worse with each pitch Timothy threw. By the end of the second inning he had given up seven runs before the manager came out to the mound with the catcher. Coach Williams asked, "What's going on?"

"I don't know," Timothy said. "I'm just a little rusty."

"How's your arm feel?" Coach Williams asked.

"It feels great," Timothy lied.

"Well, forget about the score and just throw strikes," Coach Williams said, and he walked off the field.

Timothy gave up two more runs that inning before Coach Williams pulled him out of the game. Timothy walked off the field angrily and threw his mitt at the dugout wall. Coach Williams walked up to him and said, "Don't worry about it. It's your first game back. Keep focused and you'll get another start in a few days."

Timothy nodded, sat on the bench, and watched his team lose fourteen to three. All along he masked the pain in his arm.

After he got back to his room he slammed his door, then iced his arm down in terrible pain. After three days he tried to throw the ball at practice and could barely get it to the plate. Coach Williams, busy with other players, barely noticed. Timothy made two more painful starts and embarrassingly gave up six runs in each of the first innings.

After the third game, Coach Williams approached Timothy in the locker room afterward and asked, "How are you feeling?"

"I feel fine," Timothy said. "It's just going to take me a little while to get back into my groove."

Coach Williams said, "Son, I've been a coach for over twenty years and I know when I see a player in pain. I'm cancelling your next start until you go back to the doctor and have him take a look at that arm."

"No, coach," Timothy pleaded.

"If you keep pitching in pain like this you could ruin your arm and never pitch again," said Coach Williams. "I want you in Dr. Mackenzie's office tomorrow morning. Don't worry about getting an appointment. I'll take care of it."

Timothy slammed his locker and didn't answer him.

Roberta drove to the college and took Timothy to Dr. Mackenzie's office the next morning. Dr. Mackenzie told Timothy he wanted to run some more tests on his elbow during the week. Timothy was unapproachable the entire week as he awaited the test results.

A week after the tests were taken, Roberta drove to the college again, and went to Dr. Mackenzie's office with Timothy. Dr. Mackenzie came in holding the results and said, "It's just as I thought. I'm afraid your arm hasn't healed as well as we would've liked. Another operation is a possibility, but I don't believe you'll ever be able to pitch again. As I told you before the operation, your chances were only seventy-five percent to have a complete recovery."

"You'll have to operate again!" Timothy demanded.

Dr. Mackenzie lowered his voice and said, "Timothy. Nothing would please me more than to see you get on that mound again. Your injury was quite severe. Even if I did operate on you again, you still would never be able to pitch at that level again. Over the years you've pitched so much that you damaged the nerve. I was hoping you'd be in that seventy-five percent that will fully recover, but unfortunately it looks like you won't. I'm sorry to be so blunt, but I have to face the facts and so do you."

"I won't give up," Timothy raised his voice and said. "We'll get a second opinion."

"You're welcome to do that," Dr. Mackenzie said. "I have no choice but to recommend to Coach Williams that he not let you pitch again."

Timothy's heart dropped to the floor. He fumed, unable to say a word. Roberta quickly said, "Thank you," and the doctor left the room.

Roberta went to Timothy and tried to hug him. Timothy put his hands up and said, "Don't!"

Roberta said weakly, "We can try a second opinion but you may have to take his advice."

"I won't," Timothy said. "I never will."

Two weeks later Roberta and Timothy went to another doctor for a second opinion. Dr. Fisher reviewed Timothy's case and test results. He walked into the room and asked him a few questions. Then he said, "I know you're looking for me to say that we should operate again and everything will be fine. It's my opinion that it would do very little good. In time your arm will heal and you should have very little pain, but I believe there is significant nerve damage that can't be repaired well enough for you to be able to pitch at that level again. I'm sorry."

Timothy clenched his fist and said, "No."

"I'm afraid that's the truth," said Dr. Fisher.

Roberta's eyes misted. She felt horrible that her son's life-long dream had come to an end and didn't know what to say. Finally she said, "Right now all we can do is pray and put our faith in above."

"You've been telling me that my whole life and I'm tired of it," Timothy said.

"Timothy," Roberta said. "I won't have any of that. You know better. Besides, it's not the end of the world. You're still an excellent student. You could always come back to the farm."

Timothy angrily grabbed his coat, walked out of the room and got into the car. He barely said a word the entire way back to his room. He just stared out the window. When it was time to go Roberta said, "Son. Please understand that this is His will and not to fight it."

"His will," Timothy said. "I'm supposed to be a baseball player and I will be."

"No, Timothy," Roberta calmly disagreed. "You're supposed to be a man and a man doesn't complain. A real man does what he has to when life gets tough, like your father."

Timothy said, "Please, leave me alone. I just want to be alone."

"Remember what I said about your destiny and think about coming back home," Roberta said. "And if you need to talk, call me any time."

"Oh boy," Alexander said. "I hope he went back to the farm."

"He didn't," Andrew said. "Just watch."

Throughout his senior year of college, Timothy grew more and more bitter because his lifelong dream to become a professional baseball player was now gone. Many nights he sat and brooded about his life, wishing he could get back on the mound. He felt like it was his destiny to be a star in the major leagues, but now he was left with nothing but resentment. He felt cheated.

He had to start over with no idea what he was going to do next. He knew one thing for sure, though — he didn't want to go home and be a farmer. He became withdrawn and rarely talked to his family despite Roberta's and Gerald's constant phone calls. He always had an excuse as to why he couldn't talk.

Back home, Gerald was struggling to keep the farm going and barely getting by. The fact that he didn't have Timothy's help anymore took its toll on him emotionally. He was overworked and getting up in age, and he rarely had a moment to spare. Markus and Cindy helped as much as they could, but it wasn't the same as having his strong son there who knew the farm inside and out like he did.

Timothy graduated and spent the summer working at the college without even one trip home. He started graduate school in the fall to get his master's degree in finance, and during his first year of graduate school, he got in with the wrong crowd.

"You know what happens when you get involved with the wrong people," Andrew said. "You become just like those people."

Timothy began to drink all the time and experimented with drugs. Before long he developed a taste for beer that he seemingly could never quench. He struggled in school, but managed to get by. His contact with his parents was rare and only when Gerald and Roberta initiated it. Timothy dated a few women in his first year of graduate school, but they were nothing more than flings.

In his final year of graduate school, everything changed. He met a fellow student named Josh Bandy. Josh came from a wealthy family in Boston, where his father and grandfather had been in the investment business for more than fifty years. Josh was going to be a third-generation stockbroker. Timothy and Josh hit it off immediately and became close friends.

"It's funny how people come in and out of your life all the time," Alexander said.

"As I said, everyone comes into your life for a reason, whether good or bad," Andrew said.

Josh and Timothy were inseparable during their final year of college. When they graduated, they decided to move to New York City to start out as traders on the floor at the New York Stock Exchange. Josh's father used his pull to get them the jobs because he thought it would be a good learning experience for them to start out at the bottom.

After they were fully trained, their job consisted of buying and selling orders that came up on a computer screen for their brokers on the main floor of the exchange. They had to make split second decisions when to sell and buy with thousands of dollars on the line. The job was extremely stressful with no room for error or indecision.

One day, after several months on the trading floor, Timothy was looking at his computer screen and yelled in an order: "Seven thousand Big Blue at forty-six, sold!" Finally the order came through and he was pleased. A split second later he yelled, "Five thousand shares at fifty-three UPS. I'm out. Two thousand shares Apple three twenty-three, I'm in. Seventeen hundred Kellogg, sixty-eight, I'm in." Timothy loved the feeling of executing a trade at the precise time to make the most money. The thrill and excitement reminded him of being on the mound when people used to cheer and scream for him.

"Wall Street," Alexander said. "I don't like where this is going. You know what happens to some people there. They start to love money, get enticed by its power, and they can never get enough. They end up miserable, unhappy, and lonely."

"Yes, we've seen it happen many times," Andrew said.

Timothy was about to place another order when a clerk came over to him and said, "You have an emergency call. I told them you were busy, but they said it was urgent. It's from your mother."

"I can't leave now," Timothy said. "Tell her I'll call her in an hour when the session is over."

After he was done, he returned the call. "Hi Mom, what's up?"

Roberta was hardly able to speak. "Your father had a heart attack out in the barn today. They don't think he's going to make it through the night. I'm at the hospital right now, waiting for the doctor to come and talk to me."

Stunned, Timothy said, "I'll be home as soon as I can, I promise. I'll catch the next flight out."

As it turned out, he arrived in Wisconsin early the next morning. He went directly to the hospital, where he found his brother, sister, and mother all in tears. He ran to his mother, hugged her, and asked, "How's Dad? Can I see him?"

Roberta said, crying, "Tim, he died an hour ago."

For the first time in years, Timothy cried too. Despite the resentment he felt for his father, Timothy still loved him. His mouth dropped open and his face went blank as he realized that he could never speak with him again. Timothy had so much frustration bottled up inside, and now he would never be able to make amends with his father and release it.

"Gerald was a good man," Andrew said. "That's why he's with us now in heaven."

"So young," Alexander said. "And he had a family too."

Andrew gave Alexander a sharp look. Alexander added, "Don't worry, Andrew. I know better than to question why things like that happen."

Roberta, trembling, looked up and prayed: "Please help us get through this and help Gerald enter your kingdom. He was a good man and always did your will."

Timothy sniffled and said, "He can't be gone, he can't be." He spent the rest of the day in complete denial that his father was really gone.

Two days later at the funeral home, Roberta walked into the room where Gerald was laid out and broke down when she saw him in the casket. She called up every ounce of faith she had as she prayed, *I believe you had a good reason for taking Gerald. Please help me. I hurt inside so much. Please come to me and help me.*

Timothy went up to the casket and cried as he knelt. He prayed, *God, I know I'm not the most faithful man in the world, but please help my father and especially my mother.* He continued to pray a couple more minutes and left the room.

After they attended the funeral, Roberta asked Timothy, "Is there any way you can stay for a while and help me with the farm, just until I can get things in order? Markus, Cindy and her fiancé are planning to pitch in as well."

"I can't," Timothy said. "I have to get back to New York by Monday morning. The exchange is so competitive that they'll replace me on the spot if I don't show up. You don't know what it's like."

Roberta's heart felt cold and she looked away. "That's all right. We'll manage. Don't worry about it."

"You're kidding me! Alexander asked. "Tell me he didn't go back to New York."

"Oh, he went back," Andrew said. "And he left his brother and sister behind to run the farm. They struggled terribly."

When Timothy got to his apartment he felt horrible. *First I hurt my arm, and now this. Why does life have to be so unfair? I can't believe Father is gone. If I could talk to him one more time, I'd tell him how I feel. I wish he knew that I didn't mean to be such an idiot when I was younger; now he'll never know how sorry I am. He did care about Cindy and Markus more than me though. I guess they were his favorites. No matter what I did, they were the ones that he cared about.*

After the initial days of depression, Timothy resolved to pour himself into his work to forget about the past, and over time, the pain slowly faded. He decided to start his own investment firm, thinking, *If I can't get prestige from playing baseball, then I'll get it from becoming wealthy. I'm going to make a name for myself. People are going to realize that I still have extraordinary talent.*

About six months after he started his firm, he got a phone call from his sister.

"Tim," Cindy said. "I'm calling to let you know that Mama passed away in her sleep last night. We need you to come home right away."

Timothy's mind went blank. He set the phone down and cried like a child. He cried because he loved his mother and because he felt so guilty for having deserted her. It had been over a year since he'd last seen her, after his father's funeral, and several months since he'd spoken with her.

He returned home right away. When he arrived, Cindy hugged him as hard as she could. Markus was there and joined in, and they all cried. Cindy said, "All the arrangements have been made. Visitation is tonight." Timothy, Cindy and Markus spent the day together.

When Timothy arrived at the funeral home, he found nearly a hundred people coming and going, mostly from Roberta's church. He was so distraught that he almost couldn't go into the viewing room; the guilt had been overwhelming from the moment he had heard the news. His stomach turned as he walked up to the casket; he wished he was someone else. He looked at his mother lying there and broke down. Tears rolled down his cheeks as he prayed in front of the casket. *I am so sorry, Mama, for not being there for you. I love you. Please forgive me.*

He couldn't take it anymore and left the room; for more than an hour he was unable to bring himself to return, sitting in an outer hall by himself. Finally he went back in, feeling more guilty than he ever had in his life.

During the funeral, he struggled with his guilt, weeping twice. Afterwards, he was so filled with anger that he looked for anyone to blame but himself.

That night he kicked the dresser in his old room and felt more lonely than he ever had in his life. He wished he could hide under a rock, never to be seen again. He looked up toward the heavens and said, "Is this your mercy and grace that my parents talked about my entire life? Then I don't want it. My father and mother were good people and it ends with them dying so young. It's not right! Leave me alone!"

The next day, Cindy said to Timothy, "You need to come home and help us work the farm. Mama had some life insurance, but it isn't nearly enough. Now that Bill and I are married, we can devote more time to the farm, but we need your help. Can you stay?"

"I can't," Timothy said. "I have a business to run, and I'm struggling as much as you are. I haven't been able to make my firm profitable yet and I'm close to losing everything. You have to understand my point of view."

Cindy, disgusted, said, "Oh, your investment business! I'm sure you'll want your share of the life insurance money right away, too."

"I didn't even think of it," Timothy said. "But yeah, I could use it right now."

"What's wrong with you?" Cindy asked.

"You have to understand that I have my own life now," Timothy said.

"You go ahead and go back to your business," Cindy said. "I'll try to save the *family* business, the one that supported you growing up." Then she walked away.

❧ 4 ❧

Cindy and her husband applied for another mortgage on the property. When they got the loan, they paid off Timothy's share of the inheritance and still had a little left over to keep the farm going. Timothy put the cash into his firm, working day and night to build his clientele. He managed to secure two major clients, which was a huge boost for him. He was still struggling, but at least he was able to keep his doors open.

Within a year, Cindy called Timothy and said, "I need your help. I need to raise twenty-five thousand dollars or we're going to lose the farm."

"Can't you take out a mortgage like Dad always did?" Timothy asked.

"Bill and I already did." Cindy said. "The price of milk dropped and we've tried everything."

"I don't have the money," Timothy said. "I'm barely able to pay my rent."

Crying, Cindy said, "I know you hate this farm and I know how you feel about Markus and me. But this farm has been in our family for generations. Please, help us Timothy, please."

"I don't hate the farm," Timothy said. "It's just – what can I do? I don't have the money. I'm sorry, Cindy."

Cindy wept, "Oh Tim. What am I going to do?"

"I don't know."

As he hung up, Timothy had a lump in his throat and a weak feeling in his stomach. He flashed back to when he was eight years old and helping his father milk the cows. With a slight smile, he thought about when he was seven and took the strawberry pie for which his father punished him. Then he remembered pitching at the tree he used to practice at. His anger returned as he remembered how his father used to show more affection toward Markus and Cindy.

Just then the phone rang. Timothy said "Fletcher Equities. How may I help you? Yes, I'm Timothy Fletcher. Yes, I can set up an appointment for Friday, Mr. Hendrix. Ten o'clock will be fine. I'll be here. Thank you and good-bye."

Yes, Timothy thought. *I needed that. If I can sign him, I'll be on my way. I need to prepare right away.*

Six months later, Cindy and Bill lost the farm to foreclosure. When Timothy got the news, he felt depressed at first. He poured himself into his business to mask the guilt he felt.

A little while later, the stock market boomed. For a short while, it seemed that Timothy was on fire. Every stock he picked went straight up. Suddenly everyone wanted to invest with his firm. He signed several big investors and his lust for money increased.

"Timothy stepped over the line because of his desire to make more money," Andrew said. "Watch, Alexander, this part is crucial."

One day, Timothy got a phone call from his long-time friend Josh Bandy.

"Hey buddy!" Josh said. "I haven't heard from you in a while. I hope things are going well."

"It's been pretty hard lately," Timothy said. "I lost both my parents a while back."

"Sorry to hear that," Josh said. "I hope the business is going well at least."

"It's going pretty good," Timothy said. "You know how hard it is starting from scratch. I have to say though that we've done well in equities."

"It's a dog-eat-dog world out there," Josh said. "I'm calling because I have some information that you might be interested in. I have a line on a sweet deal that we can get into. It's a takeover that's going to happen soon, and if we buy at the right time, we can make a lot of money. It's going to cost you twenty-five thousand up front. What do you think?"

"Insider trading, huh?" Timothy said. "I don't know. That's illegal."

"Oh, come on," Josh said. "Everybody does it. Do you want to work out of that little office your entire life, or do you want to move up to a luxury penthouse like I have? No one will ever know."

"I guess it wouldn't hurt just this one time," Timothy said. "I'll wire the money later today. Let me know the second you hear anything."

"Will do," said Josh. "Oh, by the way, the money has to be wired into a separate account so there's no trace. I'll send you the information. This is going to make us both rich, my friend."

"He did it, didn't he?" Alexander asked.

"Yes, he did," Andrew said. "Timothy made a lot of money off the deal, and it started him on a downward spiral. He made three more insider deals that year, and almost overnight he became a millionaire."

Alexander and Andrew watched as Timothy walked into a car dealership. He approached the salesman and said, "I'd like to look at that BMW over there in the corner."

"Wise choice," the salesman said. "It's the Series 3 coupe. Let me go get the keys."

Timothy test drove it, came back five minutes later and said, "It's all right. I'm looking for something a little flashier though."

They walked over to the front of the dealership and the salesman said, "This is one of our top of the line models. It's a Series 6 convertible coupe. It's expensive, but worth every penny. This one is about ninety thousand."

He test drove the car and fell in love with it. His desire for material things was increasing with each additional dollar he made. He said, "I'll give you one-seventy for two of them."

The salesman's eyes bugged out and he said, "You got yourself a deal."

Timothy told the salesman, "I'll take a red one and a black one. Give me the total and I'll have my secretary bring over a check tomorrow."

The salesman said, "Yes sir, right away."

Timothy grinned ear to ear. He loved the respect and the attention people gave him when they realized he had money. He thought, *This is even better than when I used to pitch back in college. You can get all the respect you want with the stroke of a pen if you have money.*

The two angels continued to watch as Timothy walked into an upscale bar and ordered a drink. A beautiful woman approached him and they talked for a while. He followed her back to her apartment, where they spent the night together. After he got home he thought, *I like not having to go through all the games and responsibilities of having a serious relationship. Besides, I don't have time for that. I'm going to build my business and when people hear my name they'll be begging me to take them on as a client.*

She was the first of many women Timothy was with, no strings attached.

Alexander shook his head in disgust. "His sins are great and he'll have to pay for them. Are you sure he isn't too far gone toward the other side?"

"Anyone can come back to us at any time," Andrew said. "It's never too late."

About six months later, Timothy's picture appeared on the cover of a well-known financial magazine with the headline, "New Kid On The Block: Fletcher Equities is one of the fastest growing small investment firms in New York." As a result, the firm's business tripled.

Not long after, Timothy received a phone call from his sister. He hadn't spoken to her since the farm had been foreclosed on.

"Timothy, we saw your magazine story and we were so proud! We wanted to let you know that you have a niece now. Her name is Jessica. We named her after Bill's aunt."

"Wow, that's great," Timothy said. "You should've called me. I should really come see her sometime. If you want to set up a college fund for her, I can help. It's never too early to start saving."

Cindy's voice grew weak and she said, "I know you're doing really well these days, but Bill and I have come into a hardship. Bill was laid off from his job and I was wondering if you could lend us some money. We'd sign a note, of course, and pay it back as soon as we can."

"How much do you need?" Timothy asked.

"Twenty-five thousand should hold us for the year," Cindy said. "We're about to lose our house. I hate to ask, but we have nowhere else to go, Tim."

"I'll wire you the money tomorrow," Timothy said. And he did.

"I knew there had to be some good in him," Alexander said enthusiastically. "He couldn't be all bad."

Andrew was less impressed. "Twenty-five thousand is a mere drop in the bucket compared to what he had at that point. He should've given her ten times that much, and it should've been a gift, not a loan."

Timothy hired as his assistant a man named Randy Williams, whom he knew from college and who was now well seasoned in investing. He had been hired at an investment firm in New York shortly after he and Timothy graduated, taking the job for low pay at first to get experience. Timothy stole him from the firm he was working at with a juicy salary and a promise of raises in the future.

Timothy's motto was, "If you only hire the best, then you will be the best."

With his thirtieth birthday approaching, Timothy decided to take a vacation. He went to an exclusive Miami Beach resort called The Palms to spend a week. He stayed in constant contact with his assistant while he was away.

Timothy was walking from the beach to his car when a woman near him dropped her suntan lotion. He bent down to pick it up, and when their eyes met, he was caught off guard by her beauty. In her ocean-blue eyes he could see the kind of sincerity that had been missing from every date he'd ever been on with a woman. She was five feet five inches tall, with medium-length strawberry blonde hair. She was fit and trim and seemed almost like a model with her tanned skin from the intense Miami sun.

He found his voice. "Excuse me, miss. You dropped this." He handed her the lotion and, unwilling to let her walk away, added, "Do you live around here?"

The woman looked him up and down, perhaps taking in his fit, athletic build and still-handsome features. "Oh no," She responded. "I'm on vacation. I live in New York state."

"I'm from New York City," Timothy said, surprised.

"I'm from Albany."

"My name is Tim Fletcher," he said, offering his hand to shake.

"Frances Blake, I'm pleased to meet you."

"I hope you don't think I'm being too forward, but would you like to have dinner with me tonight? That is, if you're single?"

"I'm single," Frances said. "But I don't know about dinner. I'm not in the habit of going out with people I don't know. I guess I could meet you at the restaurant in our hotel with a couple of my friends, if that's okay."

"That would be great!" Timothy said. "Tell me when and where."

"Let me write it down," Frances said. She found a piece of paper in her purse, scribbled an address, and told Timothy to meet her there at seven.

After Frances left, Timothy was excited. He hadn't felt that good about meeting someone in his entire life. He went back to his hotel and got a haircut, showered and shaved. He even sent his pants out to get them cleaned and pressed.

At seven o'clock, Timothy went to the Raleigh Resort in South Beach as he had agreed. He was used to speaking to important people frequently and never got nervous; he had met many women in bars before and was usually able to win them over easily. This time his stomach was doing flip-flops and he was sweating a little as he walked in.

The hostess showed him to where Frances and her two friends were waiting. "This is Monica and Kelly," said Frances, "and this is Tim Fletcher." Kelly winked at Frances in approval and Timothy caught it.

He felt confident and said, "Nice to meet you."

After Timothy sat down he asked, "So what brings you here to Miami Beach? It's a wild place and I wouldn't expect to see three ladies like you all together without dates."

"I'm engaged," Kelly said. "My fiancé is at home working. We all decided to get away for a while."

"I have a boyfriend too," Monica said. "Frances is the only one not seeing anyone." Frances gave Monica a harsh look and looked back shyly.

"So what do you girls do for a living?" Timothy asked.

"I'm a paralegal," Kelly said.

"And I'm a nurse," Monica added.

Timothy turned to Frances and she quickly avoided the subject by asking, "So what do you do for a living?"

"I own my own investment firm in New York City," Timothy said proudly. "It's very stressful but very rewarding." Monica's eyes widened and she looked at Frances coyly.

At that, Timothy's stomach settled. His confidence built and he and the three ladies talked and laughed over dinner for nearly two hours.

After dinner, Frances and Timothy went for a walk along the moonlit beach.

"So what do you do for a living?" Timothy asked. "You never said when we were eating."

"I'm a teacher," Frances said. "I teach fifth grade at Hoover Elementary School near Albany."

"That must be a lot of fun."

"Sometimes," Frances said. "At other times, it's a lot of work. You want to connect with every student you can, but some students are difficult to reach. If you get a kid with a lot of family problems or if they're uninterested in school, you really have to work hard to try to help them."

"That would've been me," Timothy said. "I didn't have much interest in school until college."

"You said you owned your own investment company," Frances said. "Is that interesting?"

"Sometimes, I guess," Timothy said. "You know, stocks, bonds, all that stuff."

"I don't know much about all that," Frances said. "Is it difficult?"

"It can be," Timothy said. "Everyone's happy if you're making them money and angry when you're not. The key is not to make any bad decisions. That's easier said than done, though."

"It sounds like you enjoy your work, like I do," Frances said. "Teaching is my passion and I absolutely love helping kids."

Timothy looked in Frances' eyes and saw a caring, loving, complete woman, different from the women he was used to seeing. She seemed unaffected by wealth, not the kind who would throw herself at him just to get her hands on his money.

"I do like my work, for the most part," Timothy responded. "The downside is that there's a lot of pressure involved."

"I guess every job has its ups and downs," Frances said.

"Yeah," Timothy said nervously. "Look, I'm leaving tomorrow, but I was wondering if I could get your number and maybe we could go out again sometime. You said you don't make a habit of going out with people you don't know. Well, now you know me." Timothy's heart raced hoping she wouldn't brush him off.

Frances smiled and said, "Sure." She reached into her purse and handed him a business card. Timothy glanced at it, then gave her one of his own.

"Frances seems like a good woman," Alexander said. "I like her. Is she who Timothy ends up marrying?"

"You know how a good woman can change a man's life," Andrew said. "Look at Roberta and how supportive she was of Gerald. A good wife is a blessing sent from above. You also know that a bad husband can make a good woman turn to the other side."

"I hope Timothy turns into a good man instead of turning her into a bad woman," Alexander said. "Somehow, though, I think he must be headed for deep trouble, or I wouldn't be here."

"You have no idea," Andrew said. "You have no idea."

5

The two angels watched as Timothy and Frances dated for a few months. Timothy would often drive to Albany to see her, and when her school schedule allowed, Frances would travel to the city to spend a few days with him.

At dinner one Saturday evening she said, "You told me that you used to go to church every Sunday when you were a child. What made you stop going?"

Uncomfortably, Timothy replied, "I don't know. When I was younger my father used to force me to go. That, and I'm so busy."

"You should start going again with me," Frances said. "I think you'd like it."

On the spot Timothy said, "Maybe I'll go with you next time I'm up here on a Sunday."

"Good," Frances said. "We could even go on a Saturday afternoon."

"Yeah, maybe."

"I haven't missed church more than two times over the last year," Frances said. "I love going."

She thought: *He's such a nice guy, so much nicer than anyone I've ever met. It's as if he's hiding something from his childhood. At times he's so intimate and at others he's distant. I like him a lot, and I can't keep being so picky. I've found fault in every man I've dated. I hope he's the one I've been waiting for.*

"Do you ever think of having children?" she asked.

"Sure. I definitely want at least two," Timothy said.

Frances felt relieved and said, "Me too."

"I hope I get at least one boy," Timothy said. When she looked at him strangely, he quickly added, "I mean, I'd be happy with boys or girls. It's just... I hope someday that I'll be able to teach my son how to play baseball. My father didn't spend much time with me when I was little and I had to learn on my own. I'm not going to do that when I have children."

Frances smiled and felt great inside. She thought, *That was the perfect answer. Timothy seems like he'd be a good father and I think I'm in love. He's almost everything I've ever wanted in a man.*

"I don't understand why you weren't married before," Timothy said. "I mean, you're beautiful and smart. I think any guy that ever went out with you would've been stupid to let you go."

She blushed a little. "I don't know. A lot of the guys I dated were jerks. That, and I just haven't found the right one yet."

Timothy thought, *I hope I'm the right one.* He looked into Frances' eyes; his heart fluttered and he knew she was the one for him. He moved closer to Frances and kissed her lips as he had many times before. They held hands until the food came, and the rest of the evening went blissfully well.

When they ended up at Frances' house, she asked, "Do you want to come in?"

"Sure," Timothy said.

They sat on the couch and watched TV and started kissing heavily. Timothy made a move and Frances pushed him away. "I'm sorry. I can't. When I'm married and have a ring on my finger then I will give myself to my husband fully. My faith won't allow it."

"I understand," Timothy said. "It's just...I think I love you."

"I love you too," Frances said. They kissed again and spent the next two hours talking. Timothy drove home late that night as he often did when he came to see her.

The next two times Timothy came to visit Frances he brought her expensive gifts, first a watch and then a pendent. The third time he showed up with a present in hand, she said, "You give me too many expensive gifts. I can't accept them anymore."

"I love giving you nice things," Timothy said. "It makes me feel good."

"I don't care about expensive things," Frances said. "I just enjoy being with you."

"Open it," Timothy said.

"Please, no," Frances answered.

"Here," Timothy said. "I'll open it." He opened it and it was a very expensive necklace. "The next time we go out you can wear it."

"I don't want it," Frances said. "Take it back and save your money. I'm just happy you're here."

"Are you sure?" Timothy asked.

"I'm positive," Frances answered.

Timothy put the necklace in his pocket and frowned, but enjoyed the rest of the evening with her anyway.

About two months later Timothy called Frances and asked, "Can you drive to the city tomorrow? I made plans for us to go out."

"Where are we going?" Frances asked.

"It's a surprise," Timothy said.

"I guess I could drive there this time," Frances said. "I'll be there at about ten o'clock tomorrow morning.

"Great," Timothy said.

Timothy got up early and spent four hours in his office compiling information for prospective clients, getting home just after ten o'clock. Frances drove up right when Timothy was getting out of the car. "Good morning," Frances said. "Where were you?"

"Oh, I just ran out for a minute to the store," Timothy said. "Hey, I have a great day planned for us. First we'll go to the park and go for a long walk. Then we'll go to the movies and out to dinner afterward."

"On the phone you sounded like we were going to do something different today," Frances said.

"Let's just play the day out and see what happens," Timothy said.

When they were at the park Timothy's phone rang. He looked at the number and said, "Sorry, babe. I have to take this." Frances waved signaling that it was fine.

Timothy talked for nearly half an hour and came back to where Frances was sitting. Timothy came up to Frances and grabbed her and hugged her. He said enthusiastically, "I just got one of the biggest clients I've ever had. I've been trying to get this guy for over a year. Yes!"

Frances said, "Congratulations."

"We're going to celebrate tonight," Timothy said. "You deserve the best and you're going to get it."

"It's all right," Frances said. "We don't need to do anything special."

That night Timothy and Frances went to one of the finest restaurants in New York City named Per Se. Timothy made sure there were beautiful roses at their table and musicians playing romantic music throughout the evening.

Timothy behaved nervously for most of the night. Finally, with a knot in his stomach, he got down on one knee and said, "I love you, Frances. You're the most beautiful woman in the world. I want to spend the rest of my life with you. Will you marry me?" He pulled out a huge diamond ring and held it before her waiting for an answer.

Frances' eyes filled with tears as she said, "I love you too. Yes, I'll marry you."

Timothy yelled, "Yes!" Everyone at the restaurant clapped and they celebrated long into the night.

The next day, Timothy sat down with Frances and said, "I've got it all figured out. You can quit your teaching job and move to New York City. I can support you, and you can be a stay-at-home mother when we have children. My business is thriving and you don't really need to work."

Frances frowned. "Give up teaching? But I love to teach. I can move to the city with you, but I don't want to give up helping children."

"We'll have enough money," Timothy said. "You don't need to worry."

"It's not about the money," Frances insisted. "It's my passion to help children."

"You can get a job at one of the schools near my house," Timothy replied.

Frances said, "All right. After we're married, we'll live at your house and I'll look for a teaching job there."

Timothy nodded and said, "You'll be happy there; you'll see."

About a week later Timothy called Frances and said, "I'm sorry, hon. I can't make it there tomorrow. It was a bad day in the market and I've had the worst time catching up. I had a new client ask to meet tomorrow and I can't cancel."

"But tomorrow is Saturday," Frances said. "I was looking forward to seeing you."

"I'm sorry, honey," Timothy said. "Will you let me make it up to you on Sunday?"

"Sure," Frances said. "You know how we talked about you going to church with me, well Sunday would be perfect."

Timothy swallowed hard and said, "All right. I'll go with you Sunday at noon. We can go out to lunch afterward." Just then his office phone rang, so he said, "I have a call I have to take. I'll see you Sunday. I love you."

"I love you too," Frances said.

On Saturday, Frances went out to lunch with Monica and Kelly. After they ordered their food Kelly said, "What's wrong, Frances? You seem a little down."

"Oh it's nothing," Frances said.

"Come on," Monica said. "You're the worst liar in the world."

"I don't know," Frances said in a depressed tone. "The wedding plans are going well and Timothy has been great. He couldn't come here today because of work. Sometimes I think he cares too much about his business."

"Are you crazy?" Kelly asked. "I wish Kenny was that hard of a worker. He's been a pretty good husband so far, but at times he's so lazy. He never picks up after himself and he has a hard time making decisions. Timothy seems like he's got it all together. He's the whole package."

"I have to agree," Monica said. "You have it good. I'd marry him tomorrow if I were you, before he gets away."

"I guess you're right," Frances said. "I just wish he was more focused on church. Did I mention he's going with me tomorrow?"

"You need to stop being so picky," Kelly said. "Remember how the last two guys you dated weren't right either. I think you got a great guy this time so I wouldn't ruin it."

"She's right," Monica agreed. "You expect this perfect person that doesn't exist. Give the guy a break. Are you going to nag him the rest of his life?"

"You two are right," Frances said. "I can't wait to see him tomorrow."

The next day Timothy drove to see Frances and went to church with her. During the service, his mind started wandering: *I think I'm going to dive heavy into pharmaceuticals. I see great long-term potential growth there. I'm also going to try to get Rodgers as a client again. I'm not giving up on him.*

When church was over and Timothy was at the restaurant eating lunch with Frances she asked, "So what did you think of Saint Bernadine's?"

"It was really nice," Timothy said. "It's just… sometimes I have trouble focusing when I'm there."

With disappointment Frances said, "I was hoping you'd like it. We could go every week."

Timothy felt pressured and sighed. "I could go sometimes, when I'm here," Timothy said.

Frances was pleased, thinking, *Remember what Monica said. Nobody is perfect; give him a break. He does treat me really well and I love him.* They spent the rest of the day together.

"Here they are on their wedding day," Andrew said.

Timothy booked St. John's Cathedral, one of the finest in the state, for their wedding. St. John's was world famous and was completed in the mid-20th century. It had beautifully hand-painted religious pictures inside and the waiting rooms were huge with expensive leather furniture inside them.

Timothy knocked on the door of the room where Frances was getting ready. Frances called through the door, "Who is it?"

"It's me, Timothy."

"Don't you know it's bad luck to see your bride right before the wedding?"

"Don't be ridiculous," Timothy said. "I make my own luck. Open the door, I love you and I want to see you."

"No," Frances said. "I want you to see me in my gown for the first time walking down the aisle."

"I told you before, I make my own luck. Open up."

"Sorry, my love. You'll see me soon enough."

Reluctantly, Timothy walked away, but he wasn't happy.

Timothy paced back and forth as he waited for the wedding to start. He thought, *I hope I'm doing the right thing. I love Frances, but even the best marriages have trouble these days. No, I trust Frances completely. She's a great person and would never do anything to hurt me. I probably should've got that prenuptial agreement like my lawyer said, just in case.*

"I don't like it," Alexander said. "He's headed for a fall. His pride will be the end of him, I just know it."

"He feels invincible because his business is thriving, he's about to marry a beautiful woman, and he has hundreds of important and influential acquaintances who are attending his wedding," Andrew said. "But what you and I know is that the meek and the humble are the ones who shine here amongst us. Unfortunately he thinks he did everything on his own. He'll be given his opportunity to change, just as every man is. The question is, will he continue to be arrogant or will he repent?"

Nearly four hundred people came to Timothy and Frances' extravagant wedding and reception. The cathedral was decorated with the finest flowers money could buy. All the men in the wedding party had identical designer tuxedos made especially for the event. Timothy had spent nearly seventy-five thousand dollars on the event, and it showed.

"He could have helped the needy with that money," Andrew said. "Obviously he had other priorities." Alexander just watched and shook his head.

Timothy stood at the altar with his knees weak and his stomach turning as Frances entered the church on the arm of her father, Rick; he gazed down the aisle and thought she was the most beautiful thing he had ever seen in his life. His heart raced; with each step, Frances came closer to being his wife.

When she arrived at the altar, Timothy nervously took her hand, realizing she was trembling. When it was time for Timothy to speak his vows, he said, "I, Timothy Fletcher, take you Frances Blake, to be my partner, loving what I know of you, and trusting what I do not yet know. I eagerly anticipate the chance to grow together, getting to know the woman you become, and falling in love a little more each day. I promise to be faithful, and to love and cherish you through whatever life may bring us."

Tears were in Frances eyes as she said, "I, Frances Blake, take you, Timothy Fletcher to be my lawfully wedded husband, my constant friend, my faithful partner and my love from this day forward. In the presence of God, our family and friends, I offer my solemn vow to be your faithful partner in sickness and in health, in good times and in bad, and in joy and in sorrow. I promise to love you unconditionally, to support you in your goals, to honor and respect you, to laugh with you and cry with you, and to cherish you for as long as we both shall live."

Timothy's eyes misted as he realized that he and Frances were now one. When the priest announced, "I now pronounce you man and wife," they kissed long and passionately in relief. Everyone in the congregation clapped.

The reception was held at the Waldorf Astoria Hotel in Manhattan. Timothy had made all the arrangements himself; the reception room was decorated in Pacific blue, with expensive linen and flowers everywhere. The five-tiered cake was topped with a hand-carved and painted bride and groom. The band was one of the best in the city.

When Frances walked in, she gasped, "Wow!"

Timothy, still beaming, replied, "Only the best for my wife."

Frances liked what she heard and murmured, "Thank you."

Timothy, caught by surprise, hesitated. "No. Thank you, Mrs. Fletcher."

The reception was a complete success with everyone saying how it was the best wedding they had ever been to.

Once they were in the honeymoon suite, Timothy said, "I have something for you. He reached in his pocket and smiled confidently. Frances opened the gift and stared in amazement.

"That bracelet is made of the finest gold from Italy," Timothy said. "The diamonds are from South Africa and it was made right here in New York."

Frances looked at the floor and felt sad. "Oh Timothy, you shouldn't have."

"You don't like it do you?" Timothy asked.

"Of course I like it," Frances said. "It's just… you didn't have to buy me something this expensive."

"Hey," he joked. "With the price of gold these days, consider it an investment."

Frances felt a little put off that her husband would joke about her wedding gift but brushed it off. She said, "I have something for you too." She reached into her suitcase and pulled out an exquisite photo album decorated with gold ribbons and blue lace. "This is for you. It has every picture of us together placed perfectly and noted from the first day we met until today. I worked hours and hours on it. I hope you like it."

Timothy was puzzled and frowned. "I love it."

"You don't like it," Frances said. "I can tell."

"I do like it," Timothy said. "It's just... it's just I expected something different. I didn't expect you to make me something. It's beautiful and so are you."

The next day the newlyweds flew to Hawaii for a two-week honeymoon. Timothy had left explicit instructions that he was to be kept in the loop while out of the office, and he received at least three phone calls a day. He also spent the first two hours of the day on the computer checking client's accounts.

Two days before the trip was over Frances said, "Dear, can't you forget about work this morning? Randy has been doing well and tomorrow is our last day."

"I'll tell you what," Timothy said. "I won't go on the computer at all tomorrow. It'll be just you and me."

"Good." Frances said.

That night, after Frances went to sleep; Timothy snuck down to the lobby and worked on his computer for three hours so he wouldn't have to use it in the morning. The next morning he spent with Frances exclusively. She was pleased and thought, *I knew he would think our life together was more important than his job. It looks like he finally realized that on the last day we were here.*

After they returned home it was back to business as usual for Timothy. He worked sixty-hour weeks and spent time with Frances mainly on the weekends. Frances put in a few applications for teaching jobs, but didn't get hired for the upcoming school year.

With Timothy at work all the time, and without the thing she loved the most, helping children, Frances became depressed. After six months of marriage, she approached Timothy and said, "I really want to go back to teaching. I miss it so much and, with you gone all the time, it would do me good."

"You don't have to work you know," Timothy said. "We have plenty of money and my wife shouldn't be forced to bring home a paycheck."

"Honey, you don't understand," Frances said. "I don't care about the money. I need to do this. I loved my students and I miss them."

"Why don't you volunteer for a literacy group?" Timothy asked. "That way you could still be around children."

"That's a great idea," Frances said.

"Speaking about children," Timothy said, "we should consider starting our family. If you had a child of your own, I'm sure you'd find it rewarding."

Alexander felt a little put off at Timothy's shallowness. He was concerned that he was too far gone and maybe he couldn't win him over, so he said, "Is that all he thinks of, having children? It would be *rewarding?* Doesn't he understand it's a lifelong commitment, with a person counting on you to guide them in the right direction? I don't know about him, Andrew."

"He does have a lot to learn," Andrew replied, "and he's one of those people who just has to learn the hard way."

"I guess we could try to start a family, if you think it's the right time," Frances said.

"Why shouldn't we?" Timothy asked.

"It's a huge commitment, and with you always gone it would be difficult for me," Frances said. "Why don't you pay Randy more and let him run the business? We have plenty of money and he has proven he can do the job."

"After you have a baby, I'm sure that's what I'd do," Timothy said.

Frances hugged him, relieved that he was going to make a change.

About six months later, Frances made the long trip downtown to Timothy's office because she had some great news. She went up to Timothy's secretary, Karen, and said, "I'd like to see my husband, please."

Karen said, "I'll tell him you're here." She called back to Timothy's office and said, "Mr. Fletcher. Your wife is here to see you."

"She's here? I'm getting ready for a very important meeting," Timothy said. "Ask her if it can wait."

Frances shook her head no and Karen said, "She wants to see you right away."

Timothy sighed and said, "Send her in."

Frances, bubbling with joy, said, "I've got some great news, honey. You'd better sit down."

"What is it?"

"I'm pregnant."

Timothy's eyes lit up and he said, "Really? That's awesome. We need to celebrate. Let's go out to dinner tonight, somewhere special."

Frances frowned. "I was hoping you could take the rest of the day off and we could spend it together. You've been working so much lately, I've barely seen you."

Now Timothy frowned. "You know I can't just drop everything here. I have a very important meeting this afternoon. I've been trying to sign this client for almost a month and I think I finally got him. He's an oil investor from Texas and it would be a big boost for the firm if we had him on board."

Frances bowed her head. "I was so excited when I found out I was pregnant that I rushed right over here. If you would take the afternoon off, we could spend it like we used to, before we were married."

"I can't," Timothy said. "This client will never reschedule. But I'll tell you what — I'll make reservations at Antonio's tonight at seven. After all, it is your favorite. We'll spend the evening together and really do up the town. I'll be home by six and we'll have the greatest night we've had since the wedding. You watch. It'll be perfect. I'll see you at six."

Frances nodded and said, "All right, honey. I'll see you then."

When Frances was leaving, she overheard Timothy say to Karen, "Make reservations at Antonio's tonight at seven."

Karen said, "Sir, I probably can't get you a table on such short notice."

"Get the restaurant on the phone and I'll talk to the manager."

Frances waited outside the office and overheard Timothy say, "This is Timothy Fletcher from Fletcher Investments. Oh yes, my wife is fine. It's a very special occasion tonight and I need a table at seven. I don't care if you're booked. This is a very important evening for my wife." Frances' eyes widened.

Timothy continued, "I said, seven. I have a lot of very influential people that are my clients. I wouldn't want to tell them that you refused to serve us on the evening when we found out we're going to be parents. Yes, I will take care of you. Just have the table ready."

Frances went home in tears, wondering if she had made a mistake by marrying him. He seemed so distant now and self-centered, so different from when they first started dating. She knew being pregnant might be making her more emotional, but she was suddenly unsure of Timothy's commitment to be home once their baby was born.

She knelt at the side of their bed and prayed, "God please help Timothy stop being so distant. Help him realize that his family is more important than his job. Please help him be understanding towards my feelings. Watch over him and keep him safe, God." When she got up, she felt better, but still worried.

Timothy's meeting ran late and he didn't get home until almost seven. It was almost eight by the time they got to the restaurant. Timothy asked for the manager and said, "Tony, I'm sorry I'm late. Can you get us a table?"

"We're very busy, sir, but of course I'll see what I can do," Tony said.

"It's a special night for my wife. Don't let us down." Then he handed him three one-hundred-dollar bills.

When Frances saw this, she felt uncomfortable. She looked at Timothy and saw a different man than she had ever seen before. She was pregnant now with his child, and hoped again that, once the baby was born, he would realize that she and the baby were what was really important in his life.

Timothy soon began to feel the added responsibility of having a child on the way. He thought, *I want to provide a solid future for my wife and child. There is no way I want to live like my father did, always worrying about whether I'm*

going to be able to pay my bills. My business is doing well right now, so I'm going to work as hard as I can until the baby is born, and then cut back. If I build up enough cash in reserve, maybe I can start spending more time at home. That's what I'll do.

All through Frances' pregnancy, Timothy worked even harder to make his business prosper. With prosperity came the desire to increase his standard of living. Timothy and Frances moved to a plush apartment in New York City that would require a large, steady income to pay for.

"He's way off track," Alexander said. "He doesn't understand that all the money in the world isn't going to provide for his children if he's not there for them emotionally. It's spending time with them and teaching them right from wrong that makes a difference."

"We know that, but on earth it's easy to get distracted by worldly things," Andrew said. "How many times have we seen men on their deathbeds wishing they had spent more time with their families? I've never heard someone say they wish they had spent more time at the office."

Eight months after Frances told Timothy she was pregnant, she was rushed to the hospital.

Frances was in the delivery room for six hours with Timothy by her side. Nurse Gilbert stayed with Frances most of the time, with Dr. Hamlin coming in and out checking her progress. Finally the doctor told her, "You're almost fully dilated; that baby is coming."

Timothy's legs felt like rubber as he squeezed Frances' hand and she screamed one last time. "It's here," the doctor called out.

Timothy felt dizzy and his stomach was churning. Nurse Gilbert weighed the baby, handed the baby to Timothy and said, "It's a boy, seven pounds eight ounces. Congratulations, Mr. Fletcher. You're a father."

Timothy said, "Hi Ryan. I'm your father."

"I like that name," Alexander said. "Is his name written in the Book of Life? I hope he makes it."

"You know we don't know that yet," Andrew said. "A lot of that is going to depend on what you do to save Timothy."

Alexander looked on nervously as Timothy took a deep breath and held his son for the first time.

Timothy's heart melted and he couldn't speak. He looked into his child's eyes and a deep feeling of love washed over him. It didn't come often in his life, and he would not easily forget it.

Out of breath, Frances asked, "How is he?"

"He's beautiful," Timothy said.

"Bring him to me," Frances said.

Timothy gave Ryan to Frances and they both gazed into his eyes, losing themselves in love from the incredible miracle of life. Frances saw the expression on Timothy's face and thought that surely this would be the thing to bring her husband back to reality and help him to understand the true meaning of life.

Frances held Ryan until the nurse came for him, saying, "I have to take him to do all the preliminary checks and clean him up. He'll be in the nursery in an hour or so. You can see him then. You two can take a little more time, but it's best if you get some rest. You'll need all the sleep you can get right now."

Timothy nodded, kissed his wife, and said, "I'm going to let you get some rest. It's been a long night. Call me later, when you wake up."

Not five minutes after Timothy left her room, his phone rang. It was Randy, calling from the office. "I know you're at the hospital, Tim, but there's been a meltdown in the market. Stocks are down about three percent and falling. Curbs are in which has helped, but it looks like it's going to be a horrible day. We have investors calling us, wanting to liquidate everything. Many of them are asking to talk to you personally. What should I do?"

"Tell everyone to hold on and don't sell," Timothy said. "If they panic, it'll be much worse for them and for us. I'm leaving now. I'll be there as soon as I can."

"So much for the short-lived feeling of love that was going to change him when he held his son in his arms," Alexander said.

Timothy spent the next six hours at his desk, calling investors and calming their fears about the sudden decline in stock prices; in the long run, the brief panic didn't amount to much. When he returned to the hospital, Frances was awake and holding Ryan, and her parents were there, visiting her and their first grandchild.

Timothy leaned over to kiss her and said, "I'm sorry I couldn't get back here sooner. I almost had a catastrophe at work. Can I hold my son?"

Frances gave Timothy the baby. He sat down with Ryan, who began to cry instantly. Timothy asked nervously, "What's wrong?"

Frances smiled and said, "He's a baby. That's what babies do."

Frances' mother, Carol, showed Timothy how to calm Ryan by gently rocking him. Timothy spent the next two hours visiting his son, his wife and her parents, then got ready to go home. It had been a long day and he felt exhausted and overwhelmed.

As he made his way out, Frances' father stopped him. "Tim, can I have a word with you?"

"Sure."

As they walked down the hall together, Rick said, "I just wanted to let you know that you're a lucky man to have a beautiful, healthy son. You truly are blessed." Rick liked Timothy. He thought he was a hard-working man and knew he loved his daughter.

"I know I am, and I'm grateful," Timothy said.

"Frances is going to need your help," Rick said. "We have to go home in a few days and I worry about her being alone. Right after a pregnancy can be a difficult time for a woman. Some women start to feel isolated and depressed. Is there any way you can take some time off from the office?"

"I plan on taking off the rest of the week, after you leave," Timothy said. "It's been hectic at work, but I think I can swing it. I also plan on hiring a full-time nanny to help Frances out. We can afford it."

"She really needs *you*," Rick said. "The birth of a child is one of the most joyous times in a couple's life. It should bring the two of you closer together. Don't miss out on it."

"I won't," Timothy promised.

Frances' mom and dad stayed for three days helping out and then left. Timothy took a week off work to help with

Ryan and to make sure Frances was well rested. On the first day Frances said, "I'm going to teach you how to feed Ryan just in case I'm not here."

"Not here," Timothy said. "What do you mean?"

"You're going to have to watch Ryan on your own sometimes, silly," Frances said. "Sit down in the chair." She handed Ryan to him and said, "This is how you hold him. You have to keep his head supported."

Timothy looked at Ryan all swaddled up in his blanket and smiled. He was nervous and unsure of himself, but felt the warmth from the love for his son throughout his body. Ryan started to fuss and broke into a slight cry. Timothy panicked and asked, "What's wrong?"

"Nothing's wrong," Frances said. "He's hungry." She handed Timothy the bottle and said, "You hold the bottle in one hand and gently wait for him to take it. That's it."

Ryan took the bottle and started sucking on it. Timothy smiled and said, "Wow! This isn't so hard."

"See, you're a natural," Frances said.

Ryan drank almost the entire bottle and then started fussing again. "What's wrong now?" Timothy asked.

"He needs to be burped," Frances said. "Take him over your shoulder like this and lightly pat his back." Timothy did and Ryan let out a small burp. Two seconds later he let out another one. Frances laughed and said, "See, he's just like his father."

Timothy smirked and said, "Hey! He is just like his father." Frances looked at Timothy and Ryan and was glowing. All her hopes and dreams in life apparently had come true; Timothy would now be the father she wanted him to be.

A little later Frances said, "It's time for you to learn how to change him."

"I think we can leave that part to you," said Timothy.

"Oh, no," said Frances firmly. "We're in this together and you have to learn how to change him."

Frances undid Ryan's diaper and said, "Take hold of it like this." Timothy took hold of the diaper, and right then Ryan started to pee.

Timothy panicked and asked, "What do I do now?"

Frances closed the diaper back up and said, "Relax. When he's done, we'll just change his diaper." After waiting a moment, Frances helped Timothy change Ryan and then said, "See? That's all there is to it."

"I don't know," said Timothy. "What if he goes number two?"

"You'll get your chance for that soon," laughed Frances.

"I can't wait," Timothy joked.

Later that day Timothy told Frances he was going out for a walk. When he got down the street he called Randy and asked, "How did things go today?"

Randy said, "Not so great. Fred Baker closed his account. I asked him why he was doing it and he said he was going to explore other avenues."

"That's the biggest blow-off line I've ever heard," Timothy said, agitated. "Why didn't you call me?"

"I did call you," Randy said. "Your phone was off. Remember, you're on vacation."

"That's right," Timothy sighed. "I'll call him now."

He hung up and called Fred Baker and said, "I heard you closed your account with us today. Is there anything I can do to help?"

"No," Fred said. "I have something else I want to do."

"We've known each other for years," said Timothy. "You don't mind if I ask what you've got going?"

"I just wanted to pull out," Fred said. "I'll talk to you soon. Goodbye, Timothy."

When he got back into the house Frances asked, "How was your walk?"

"Oh all right," Timothy answered.

"What's wrong?"

"Nothing."

"I've known you long enough know when something is bothering you," Frances said.

"I'm a little tired," said Timothy. "Having a new son is a little more work than I thought. I'm going to lie down and take a nap."

Frances said, "You go ahead. If Ryan doesn't sleep through, we might be up all night."

Timothy thought, *Great,* and went to lie down.

Frances thought: *He seems irritated. I wonder what happened to make him feel that way after we spent the last two days together. It's been amazing. Maybe he is just tired.*

Later that night, after Ryan and Frances were asleep, Timothy went into his home office and spent three hours briefly going over all his clients' portfolios. When he was finished he thought: *When I get back to work I'm going to give a personal courtesy call to every one of my clients. I'm not going to lose another client like I lost Fred Baker.*

When Ryan was seven days old, Timothy got another phone call from Randy. "Are you watching the news?" Randy asked. "The market is dropping again and things are out of control. There's a panic on the street and we've already had Eckles and Robinson liquidate their accounts. You'd better get down here right away."

"I'll be right there."

Timothy rushed into the other room feeling sick to his stomach. His heart was beating faster and he started to sweat.

He went to Frances and said, "I have to go to the office. The market is in crisis and the future of the company is at stake. I'll make it up to you, I promise."

"Go ahead if you need to," Frances said. "It's all right. I love you."

"Timothy left, didn't he?" Alexander asked.

"Not only did he leave," Andrew said. "He went right back to his sixty-hour-a-week schedule. He did hire a nanny, which helped Frances, but it could never make up for how their relationship would've blossomed if he'd been there."

Timothy's business lost thirty percent of its value that year. He found himself ridden with worry, and rarely spent time with his wife or son. He'd stopped drinking when he and Frances started dating, but he found himself drinking again, far too often.

"Disgusting," Alexander said. "I hate to see what happens next."

"Time passes quickly and can never be regained," Andrew said. "And children grow up whether their father is there or not."

Andrew and Alexander watched as Ryan grew into a chubby toddler who took his first step without Timothy there to see it. Frances videotaped the big event so it would be preserved in time. Soon afterward, Frances found she was pregnant again.

She was full of joy at the fact that Ryan would have a brother or sister. She loved the feeling of having a new life inside of her and was thankful for the miracle of life she was given. But after she found out, she prayed, "Oh God, please help this baby be healthy like the first one, and please help Timothy be more understanding. Help him realize that his children are a blessing sent from you and that he should relish that blessing. Help him understand that I will need him more than ever and that he should be home more."

One night, after Timothy came home late from work, as usual, she told him, "We're going to have another baby."

"That's great!" Timothy said. He walked up to her, hugged her and said, "I'm going to be a father again. I love you very much. Do you know if it's going to be a boy or a girl yet?'

Frances shook her head and quickly said, "I want to talk to you about something. Since we're having another child, let's move out of the city and raise our family in the country. We don't need this expensive apartment and all these things. I want you to be here with me to see our children grow."

"I can't do that," Timothy said. "How would we survive?"

"You could open a branch office of the company in a smaller city and we could live outside the city limits. You could let Randy run your office here; you can afford to hire the very best employees and could even hire someone to help him. We could make it work, and we wouldn't need nearly as much money that way. I want our children to grow up in a better place. And I don't like how unhappy you've been lately."

Timothy said angrily, "I'm not unhappy. And as far as growing up in the country, I did that as a child and it's not all it's cracked up to be, believe me. I provide a good living for you and Ryan. Our life is here. We can't move."

"You've been gone so much lately, I feel like I hardly know you," Frances said. "Ryan is going to be two years old before long and you need to spend more time with him."

"I do spend time with my son, as much as I can. But it's critical that I get the business back on track. I have to do something to increase revenue. You don't know what it's like to be a man and have all these responsibilities."

Frances bowed her head and started to cry. "I love you, Tim, but I feel so lonely and cooped up here in the city. Please think about it."

Timothy took her by the hand and said, "I'll think about it," and left it at that.

Frances felt a little better, but not much.

"I see he's still ungrateful for his parents' sacrifices," Alexander said.

"Yes, he is," Andrew replied. "Many men can never let go of their past, and they spend the rest of their lives with bitterness inside. Bitterness will destroy a man if he can't overcome it."

"And Timothy's childhood wasn't even a bad one," Alexander said.

"Watch what happens just two months before his second child is born," Andrew said. "He should've used faith to get by."

Timothy was sitting at his desk and had just gone through all the quarterly statements that his company was going to send out to their clients. With his head in his hands, he thought, *I have to do something immediately. If I don't, I may never get out of this hole I'm in.*

He called his old friend Josh Bandy and said, "Hey Josh, it's Tim. How are you doing?"

"I've been better," Josh said. "With the economy and the market the way they are, it's hard to make a buck."

"Don't I know it!" Timothy agreed. "That's kind of why I'm calling. I was wondering if you had any more information about any takeovers coming up. My business could really use a boost."

"Well, I've got one deal in the works," Josh said. "If you want in, it's going to cost you twenty-five thousand."

"Is it big?" Timothy asked.

"Oh, it's big all right," Josh returned. "You could make a million or two, easy."

Timothy didn't hesitate. "I want in for sure. I'll have the money in the account later today. You'd better not forget about me on this one. I need it badly."

"Don't worry, Tim, you're in. One thing, though, if anyone asks, you didn't hear it from me. I'm not going down for anyone, even you. Remember, if you do this too much you'll call attention to yourself. This will be the last one for a while."

"You can count on me," Timothy said.

He made the trade at the perfect moment and his firm made over a million dollars on the deal. When he got the news, he made a fist, punched the air, looked out at the breathtaking view of the city and thought, *Yes! I'm back. I love this city and I love this job.*

Timothy took the money and paid most of it out on debts that his company had incurred in the recent downturn. And again his company appeared to be stable, at least for a while.

Two months later, while Timothy was getting ready for work, Frances came into the bathroom and said, "My water just broke. We need to go to the hospital."

Timothy immediately said, "Grab your bag. Let's go." He rushed Frances to the hospital where she spent eighteen hours in labor. He never left her side.

Finally the doctor came in and said, "I don't think we should let this go on. We've already increased the Pitocin to try to induce the birth, but it doesn't seem to be helping. I think our only option is a Caesarean section. It's a risk, but one we have to take. We're prepping the room right now."

Timothy asked, "How serious is it?"

"There always is a significant risk with any surgery," Doctor Cartwright said. "But I've performed hundreds of these, so try not to worry."

Frances said, "I'm worried. You'll stay with me the whole time, won't you?"

Timothy said, "Of course I will. There's nothing to be afraid of. You heard the doctor."

Timothy held Frances' hand as she was rushed into the operating room thirty minutes later. Timothy never left her side, and soon they had a healthy new daughter. After the nurse cleaned up the baby, she handed it to Timothy and said, "Congratulations, Mr. Fletcher. You and your wife have a beautiful baby girl."

Timothy held his daughter in his arms and savored the moment, while Frances was unconscious from the medication. He looked into his daughter's eyes and his heart fluttered. His eyes teared up for a brief moment as he felt true love, the love that only a parent could feel for a child. He said, "Ashley Fletcher, I love you."

At that moment, Timothy felt like he was being tugged in two directions. He felt that he needed to provide a living for his family, but he also felt like his time was valuable with his family. He had the gift of free will, and he was at a crossroads. He had the opportunity to turn his back on all the material things the world had to offer and follow a different path, one based on love.

His feelings were interrupted when the nurse came up and said, "I need to borrow your daughter for a bit, to make sure everything is done before she goes to the nursery." Timothy handed his daughter to the nurse, but the brief moment of bliss he'd experienced was now embedded in his mind. It would be a memory he could draw upon in times of trouble.

Andrew turned to Alexander and said, "Remember that moment. With the lifestyle he's lived, and with the other side tempting him and fighting for his soul, you may need to use it when you go down to earth. I hope he's able to remember that feeling, and that it's enough to sway him when eternal damnation is staring him in the face."

6

Andrew was about to proceed with the review when Alexander nervously said, "I hope I'm able to save him. It's been so long since I've been back to earth, and he's so lost."

"I hope so too," Andrew said. "I'm afraid the other side wants him badly and will throw everything they can at him. They're so shrewd and will stop at nothing to get him. Don't give up on him though. He is able to be saved and I have complete confidence in you."

Alexander gulped, feeling the pressure. They resumed Timothy's life review and cut right to Frances coming home from the hospital. Rick and Carol visited again; after they left, Timothy took a week off work, accepting calls at home and working out of his office there. He stayed with Frances, helping her as much as he could when he wasn't on the phone.

When Ashley was two weeks old, Frances said, "I'm feeling much better today. I was wondering if you wouldn't mind watching Ryan and Ashley for an hour. I'd like to go to the store, just to get out of the house for a while."

Timothy squirmed a little and said, "I don't know if that's a good idea with Ashley being so young."

"Nonsense," Frances said. "Ashley is asleep and Ryan just went down for his nap. I'll be back in an hour."

"If you must, then I'll have to," Timothy said.

Frances was disappointed in Timothy's lack of enthusiasm and said, "If you can run a multi-million dollar company, then you should be able to watch your own children for an hour." Timothy nodded.

About fifteen minutes after Frances left, Ashley woke up crying. Timothy picked her up and tried to comfort her. She continued to cry, so Timothy warmed up a bottle.

Ashley was used to Frances feeding her and for some reason wouldn't take the bottle at first. Timothy became frustrated and called Frances, saying, "Ashley is crying and I don't know what to do. I tried feeding her twice and she won't eat."

"I don't know why she won't eat," Frances said. "Try singing to her while you give her the bottle. I'll be home in ten minutes."

Timothy felt incompetent but held Ashley a third time and sang "Take Me Out To The Ball Game" while he tried feeding her. Now she drank the entire bottle. He burped her afterward and Frances walked in a few minutes later, asking, "Is everything all right?"

Timothy answered, "She took the whole bottle and everything is fine. I'm just not good with little babies though."

Frances' stomach went empty and she frowned. "She's your daughter and you should be able to watch her at any time."

"I will," Timothy responded. "When both the kids get older I'll be taking them to the park and everywhere. You'll see. When they're small it's so hard."

Frances felt a little better at that.

When the week was up, Timothy hired another nanny to help Frances. He went back to work two weeks after Frances came home from the hospital, and jumped right back into the grind of satisfying customers and trying to make profits. This time though, Timothy had something deep inside that was different about him: a memory of his daughter in his arms for the first time.

"Watch this, Alexander," Andrew said. "This could be important too."

When Ryan was three, Timothy called Frances and said, "Hi dear. I'm going to come home early from work. I want to take Ryan somewhere special. Have him ready at two o'clock."

Frances surprised said, "He'll be ready."

When Timothy came home he kissed his wife and said, "I would tell you where I'm taking Ryan, but it's a surprise. I should've done this long ago. My father did this for me when I was younger."

Frances, beaming with hope for the future, excitedly said, "Where are you taking him? Tell me, please."

"Oh no," Timothy said. "You'll just have to see when we get back."

It was one of the few times in the past three years that Frances had hope. She smiled confidently and felt that her man, the father of her children, was finally coming around. She got down on her knees and prayed long and hard after

Timothy left. "Oh God, thank you for making Timothy finally see how important Ryan and Ashley are. I knew you would help him eventually. I never lost faith."

Timothy drove with Ryan to a sporting goods store about five miles away. Timothy walked in and said to the man that was working there, "I'd like to buy my son his first baseball glove. He's long overdue. Can you show me something in his size?"

The man smiled at Ryan and asked, "Left-handed or right?"

Ryan shyly looked back and didn't say anything.

Timothy said, "Left."

The man walked Timothy and Ryan over to an aisle and said, "Here are all the gloves. Do you need help picking out a starter one for him?"

Timothy smiled at the man and said, "No. I played four years of college baseball. I think I can handle it."

"You played four years in college, wow," the man said. "I played high school ball and that was it. Were you any good?"

"I went sixteen and four in my junior year and was about to be drafted by St. Louis when I blew my arm out," Timothy said. "It wasn't fair. I could've been great."

"Our glory days," the man said, "if we could just go back."

A memory of being on the mound in college flashed in Timothy's head – and then a memory of his dad's broken promise to play catch with him when the tractor broke down followed, and ruined it.

The clerk said, "Well if you need me, I'll be over by the register."

Timothy smiled back. "Thanks." He picked out a nice glove for Ryan and went home.

When they got there Frances said, "I've been dying to find out where you two went."

Ryan ran up to his mother and held his glove proudly and said, "Daddy bought me a baball gwove."

Frances looked at Ryan and almost cried. With a look of pure jubilation she turned to Timothy and said, "I love you."

Timothy looked back and said, "I love you too."

Timothy spent over an hour playing catch with his son for the first time. In fact, it was really the first time in quite a while that Timothy played with Ryan as a father should. He enjoyed their time together, which seemed to pass by in a flash.

"He's looks like he's changing for the better," Alexander said.

"Oh, you think he's changing for the better?" Andrew mocked. "I wish it were that simple. You know the other side isn't going to give up on him that easily. They're going to send evil people into his life to bring him back just like we send good people all the time to help him stay on the straight and narrow. That store clerk might have seemed insignificant, but he wasn't. He made Timothy think about what's really important in life for a brief second and sometimes that's all a man needs to turn himself around. Unfortunately it's going to be short-lived. The other side will use all the stored-up resentment Timothy has towards his father against him."

Timothy's life continued to play out as the angels saw him go to church that Sunday for the first time in quite a while. When he went back to work Monday, all the financial markets across the world were up, and Timothy was enticed again with the desire for money and the power it brought.

At the end of the day Timothy received a phone call. "My name is Ken Respon and I work for James Calvin, who owns Calvin Enterprises. Mr. Calvin got your name from a friend and would like to set up a meeting with you. He's considering allowing you to take over a portion of his finances for investment. Would Wednesday afternoon be fine to meet?"

Timothy knew of Mr. Calvin, who was a very wealthy and prominent businessman. He said, "Wednesday afternoon will be fine, say around three."

"That will be perfect," said Ken Respon, and he hung up.

Timothy punched his fist in the air and cried, "*Yes.*" He called Randy and explained the situation. "I want this client at all cost," Timothy said. "Find out everything you can about Mr. Calvin and don't spare a dime. I'm going to be ready for the meeting and we're going to sign this guy."

Randy said, "Yes sir," and started gathering information about their prospective client. Timothy spent sixteen hours each of the next two days at the office and barely got to see his family. When the meeting came Timothy was totally prepared. He showed Mr. Calvin all the successes he had had in the past and very much impressed him. But Mr. Calvin wasn't one hundred percent convinced that Timothy was the right person to handle such a large amount of his money, so he said, "I'll think about it and get back with you."

After Mr. Calvin left, Timothy called Randy and said, "Find out where he's going to be tonight. I don't care if I have to walk over hot coals; I'm going to get him to sign with us."

Randy came back later and said, "He's going to be at an art opening tonight. It's an upscale event where there'll be a lot of high-priced paintings for sale."

"Get me tickets for that show," Timothy said. "I'll change Mr. Calvin's mind about having me handle his money if it's the last thing I do."

Timothy went to the art show and saw Mr. Calvin admiring a painting off in the distance. Even though Mr. Calvin could afford anything he wanted, he told the seller he thought the painting was overpriced. After Mr. Calvin moved on to the next area of the show, Timothy went over to the seller and bought the painting.

Timothy took the painting and had it hand delivered to Mr. Calvin the next day with a note that said, "Please accept this gift from Fletcher Investments. I know it was a little overpriced, but you're worth it. If I'll do this to try to get your business, just think about what I'll do to keep your business." The note was hand signed by Timothy.

Mr. Calvin was impressed by Timothy's tenacity. Mr. Calvin agreed to let him handle a portion of his finances. He wanted to let Timothy start out small, with the agreement that if he did well, his business would increase with Timothy's firm.

After Timothy got the news he yelled, "Yes! I did it!" He thought: *You have to spend money to make money. Like that time I went after Michael Hampton and found out he was a huge Yankees fan. It was brilliant how I paid a thousand dollars for two front row seats next to the dugout for him. It was worth every penny paying that usher fifteen hundred dollars to get a couple of players to come up to him and give him a ball and autograph it. If that's the way business is done, then I guess these are the things I have to do. You are a genius, Fletcher. You're invincible. You just signed James Calvin.*

Timothy smiled to himself. He loved the power that wealth gave him. He loved the fact that at almost any time he could reach into his pocket and pull out a large sum of money and solve almost any problem. He loved how he could get the best tables at restaurants, get front-row concert tickets, or even get tickets to a sold-out art event where he could buy an expensive painting and give it away.

Alexander didn't say anything. He just shook his head in disgust.

Timothy spent the next two months working harder than ever trying to make a huge profit for Mr. Calvin. He succeeded. Mr. Calvin transferred more of his finances into Timothy's company, with the agreement that Timothy would manage his assets personally. Timothy agreed.

"He's right back where he started," Alexander said.
"Yes, he is," Andrew agreed. "It gets worse; just watch."

Timothy now spent long nights at the office doing research and working harder than ever to satisfy his customers. He became obsessed again with building wealth for his clients, while Frances stayed at home, as lonely as ever, trying to raise their children.

One night, when Ryan was three-and-a-half years old, Frances was getting both her children ready for bed when Timothy came in and said, "Hello, honey. I'm home."

Frances looked at Timothy and didn't say anything.

"It was a terrible day at the office and I'm beat. How was your day?"

"It was a great day for me," Frances said. "Ashley said her first word, and of course you weren't here to hear it. Do you have to stay at work so late all the time?"

Timothy immediately went on the offensive. "Yes, I have to stay so late all the time. You know we do have bills to pay. It costs money to live in such a nice neighborhood."

Frances had had enough and was near to breaking down, but tried to hold back. She calmly said, "I don't care where we live, and I don't care about money. I care about you. Give up your business and we'll find a way to make it, please."

"Watch this," Andrew said. "It's the other side using his ego to make him angry."

Timothy raised his voice and said, "How dare you tell me what to do! I'm not giving up my business. You're not going to dictate what I do and don't do. Sometimes you can be so controlling."

That pushed Frances to her breaking point. "You're never here anymore! I can't keep this up any longer. All day long I stay at home and take care of the kids while you're out wining and dining clients. Do you know what it's like for me?"

Both Ryan and Ashley began to cry, sensing the hostility between their parents.

"Do I know what it's like for you?" Timothy yelled back. "I go to work every day and slave at the office so I can provide for you and our children and all you think about is yourself. Do you know what it's like for me worrying where my next client is going to come from? Do you know what it's like having hundreds of people depending on every decision I make? Do you realize if I make the wrong decision people's lives are affected? Your life is a walk in the park compared to mine." He turned to the couch and kicked it.

Frances turned red, began to cry and yelled back, "Get out!"

Timothy had to get the last word in. "How dare you ask me to give up my business! Who do you think you are? I'm leaving and don't expect me back tonight." He stormed out, slamming the door behind him leaving Frances, Ryan and Ashley all crying.

Frances picked up Ashley while Ryan tugged on her leg crying for attention. She sat down, held a child in each arm and comforted them, taking comfort and hope from holding them. When they had finally quieted down, she put them to bed, still upset from the terrible fight.

She prayed, *God give me strength to get through this night and help Timothy realize how lonely I am. Please bless Ryan and Ashley and help them serve you.*

Meanwhile, Timothy went to a local bar and ordered a double round of shots to start. He sat there drinking for over an hour until he noticed a woman sitting all alone at the other side of the bar. He noticed that she was quite attractive and a little younger than himself. He approached her and asked, "Can I buy you a drink?"

Startled she said, "Sure."

"I'm Tim Fletcher. I'm pleased to meet you."

"I'm Cheryl Brown."

The bartender brought their drinks and Timothy said, "What a lousy day. Everything I did went wrong. Sometimes I wish I could ride away into the sunset and never come back."

"I know what you mean," said Cheryl. "I've had a few days like that lately." They enjoyed each other's company for an hour more before Cheryl went on her way. Timothy stayed at the bar and had a few more drinks.

Timothy came home around one o'clock and slept in the other room. He got up for work just before Ryan and Ashley woke up. As he was getting ready to leave, he said, "I'm sorry about last night, dear. I was wrong. I should've never argued with you like that. Just give me a little time to get my business straightened out and I'll take some time off. Then we can spend a lot more time together."

Frances didn't say much until Timothy came up and kissed her. After that Timothy said again, "I'm sorry. Please forgive me."

"I forgive you," Frances said. "It's just that Ryan and Ashley are growing so fast and you're missing out on everything. I want them to know their father."

"And they will," Timothy said. "Give me some time. You'll see. I'm going to take the weekend off and we can go take a drive upstate where you used to live. We'll spend the whole weekend together. What do you say?"

Frances smiled and asked, "Do you promise?"

"I promise," Timothy said and then he left for work.

"Did he keep his promise?" Alexander asked.

"He kept his promise," Andrew said. "After that weekend though, things went right back to normal, with him working fourteen hours a day most of the time. It's funny sometimes how a man falls into a rut and never does anything to get himself out of it until he's pushed to the edge. Well, Timothy is going to be pushed to the edge all right, just watch."

Andrew and Alexander saw Frances and Timothy grow further and further apart; she grew even more demanding about him giving up his business. They argued constantly about the subject; whenever they were together, it seemed to end in an all-out fight. Ryan and Ashley were always the ones who suffered the most, seeing their parents act that way.

A year later, Timothy was still working himself to the bone. He had become so unhappy that he turned to prescription narcotics to bring him some relief. It was the end of the day on a Friday, and Timothy reached into his pocket and pulled out a pill. He thought about going home and facing Frances again after the fight they had had the night before. He put the pill into his mouth and took a drink of water and swallowed it. An hour later, he was completely calm when he walked into the house. He apologized to Frances, cracked open a beer and went into his private office. He watched TV for the rest of the night, completely zoned out.

"Not drugs," Alexander said sadly.

"He took a few here and there, but never overdid it at first," said Andrew. "Unfortunately it gets worse. When money is your main interest in life and it isn't satisfying anymore, people usually turn to something else. Unfortunately Timothy turned to drugs."

A year later, Ryan was five and Ashley was three. Timothy was in his office when he received a phone call. The woman on the phone said, "My name is Rachel Wilkins. I represent Angela Farnsworth from Cachet Designers. Mrs. Farnsworth would like to set up a meeting with you about possibly having your firm handle a portion of her investments."

"*The* Angela Farnsworth, the famous designer?" Timothy asked.

"Yes that's her," Rachel said. "Is tomorrow at three o'clock fine?"

"That would be perfect," Timothy said. "I'll see her tomorrow, thank you." Then he hung up the phone. Timothy called Randy and said, "I want you to find out everything you can about Angela Farnsworth from Cachet Designers. And I want the information on my desk within three hours."

"Three hours?" Randy said.

"You heard me. I don't care if you have to put three people on it. Get that information and get it fast."

"Yes sir," Randy said

Three hours later Randy came into Timothy's office and said, "I have everything you wanted."

"Well, out with it," Timothy said.

"She's thirty-five years old, very attractive. She started Cachet Design Incorporated seven years ago at the age of twenty eight. After two years, she started her own line of perfume, makeup, hair products and of course her clothing line. Her company averaged sales of one hundred million a year over the last three years. Her net worth is somewhere around one hundred and twenty-five million dollars. She likes parties, art and movies. Rumor has it she's been on the set or at the filming of a couple of major movies in the last year. She invested in a movie called *Zombies Forever* and it did pretty well. She'd definitely be a big catch if you can reel her in."

"I'll reel her in," Timothy said. "You wait and see."

The next day Angela Farnsworth came into Timothy's office as planned. She walked in with an entourage of six people. After she made her grand entrance, Timothy introduced himself and escorted Angela and her people to a conference room down the hall. After they reached the conference room, Angela told her people to wait outside and then requested to meet alone with Timothy. Timothy agreed and sent Randy to wait outside.

Angela had long blonde hair down to the middle of her back. At five feet seven inches tall, she had the body of a model. Her perfect appearance was the result of three separate visits to the plastic surgeon.

She started by saying, "I've heard good things about you from one of my buyers. He said you averaged eleven percent on his money over the last two years. I'm considering transferring some funds into an account with your company. Can you tell me what makes your company better than the hundred other firms I've considered?"

"We put our customers' needs first before anything else," Timothy said. "Besides the great return on your investment from our firm, you'll have our expertise and advice twenty-four hours a day, seven days a week. I'm available all the time."

"I see where that could come in handy," Angela said. "What about risk?"

"There's always risk involved with every investment," Timothy said. "Here at Fletcher Investments we minimize your risk by never investing in anything speculative."

"I see," Angela said. "I like you. You seem honest to me. Let's discuss this over dinner tonight at The Grommet over on Thirty-Sixth Street. Shall we say eight?"

"That would be fine," Timothy said. "Eight o'clock." Angela nodded and left after that. Timothy's mind raced and he felt full of life. He couldn't wait for the challenge to secure such a wealthy client.

He picked up the phone and called Frances and said, "Honey, I have a big meeting tonight and I won't be home until late. This is a huge chance for us and I wanted to let you know I probably wouldn't be home until after ten. Don't wait up."

"Ashley is sick," Frances said. "She came down with something today. She's running a fever of a hundred and one. It's probably nothing serious, but you never can tell. Are you sure you can't make it home early? Can't you postpone the meeting?"

"No, I can't," Timothy said. "This is a huge opportunity for me. I have to get this client. Call the doctors and see if you can get Ashley in today. Let me know if it's anything serious. If you need help, call up Consuela. She said she'd help if you ever needed her. I remember she said she could use the extra money."

"I know, but it's hard," Frances said. "Can't you cancel?"

Timothy raised his voice a little and said, "I can't. There's no way. I have to make this meeting. I'll check on Ashley when I get home. I have to go now. I love you, dear." Then he hung up without even recognizing the desperation and loneliness in Frances' voice.

Frances took Ashley to the doctor, who said it was a virus that would pass in a couple of days. Timothy spent the evening wining and dining his prospective client while

Frances stayed up a good part of the night with her sick daughter. Finally, after Frances got Ashley to bed, she was exhausted and went to sleep.

Timothy came in at two in the morning and went right to bed without waking his wife. The next morning he got up a little late; Frances was already up. She came in as Timothy was waking up and said, "It was rough last night. Ashley is doing a little better."

"Good," Timothy said. "I'm glad it was nothing serious. I'm sorry dear but I have another meeting tonight."

"Not tonight," Frances said. 'I don't think I can take another night without your help."

"I'll call Consuela and have her come over," Timothy said.

They went back and forth about it with Timothy insistent about making his meeting. It led to another argument with Timothy leaving in an uproar.

"I don't like it one bit," Alexander said.
"The worst is yet to come," Andrew said.

The two angels watched him at another restaurant that night. Angela and Timothy were talking and drinking fine imported wine. Timothy looked at Angela and felt a strong attraction to her. She was a beautiful, powerful, enticing woman. She had the love of money that Timothy had, and the wine he drank made matters worse.

Angela touched Timothy's hand and said, 'I'll transfer three million into an account tomorrow if you meet me again Friday to discuss my options."

Timothy jumped at the chance and said, "I'll meet you. Let me know when you get the funds in there tomorrow so we can get to work right away."

"My accountant will have the money there by noon," Angela said. "Don't forget, Friday night."

"I won't forget," Timothy said. They spent the rest of the evening together joking, laughing and talking about finances. Timothy got home very late once again.

The next morning Frances was angry and pleaded with Timothy again, "You're never home. I'm not going to raise these kids by myself. Please give up the business and let's move out of this city. We're stifling ourselves here. We can make a better life for the children if you'll just try."

Timothy's face turned red and he said, "Did I not give you the money to donate to that charity for children and literacy that you care about? And did I not allow you to continue putting all your effort towards your causes to help children? Well, those kinds of things take money. I work to provide for us so you can do those types of things."

"*Allow* me," Frances interrupted loudly. "You *allow* me to do things now. How dare you speak to me like that? What's happened to you? You've changed so much."

"All I'm saying is that I'm not giving up the business and that's final. You're so ungrateful. You have the nicest things and all you do is complain. Don't I provide you, Ryan, and Ashley with the best things possible? And don't you drive the finest car there is? Then stay off my back." Timothy walked out the door and slammed it behind him.

Frances went over to the couch and cried. She prayed once again. "Please help Tim. Help me, and send someone to make my husband realize what he's doing to his children and to me. Help us, please God, help us. I feel so lonely. I know you're there and I know you're listening. Something has happened to my husband and I need him to be a good father. Show your grace and answer my prayer, please." She cried for another twenty minutes.

"Oh Andrew," Alexander said. "Did he eventually come around?"

"You'll just have to wait and see," Andrew said.

Friday night came and Timothy met with Angela for dinner. After a few drinks, they were both rather tipsy. Timothy wanted to reassure Angela that she had made the right decision investing with his firm; he said, "Thanks for putting the money in the account so quickly. I've been working hard with your account and already made you one percent in just two days. There was an upturn in the market and I timed it perfectly. I have a feeling you're going to be really happy with my performance."

Angela was sitting next to Timothy and reached for his hand. She looked at him provocatively, touched his hand and said, "Whether I'm happy with your performance is yet to be seen."

Timothy, feeling the effects from the drinks, felt aroused. He looked at Angela and didn't resist and said, "Well, what did you have in mind."

Angela scooted closer to Timothy and said, "I'm the kind of woman that always gets what she wants. I've done it in business and I've done it in life. I didn't get to where I am today without taking a few risks along the way."

"I see," Timothy said. "Just how many risks are you willing to take?"

"I do whatever I want when I want," Angela said. "I enjoy life without thinking about the consequences."

"It's a good thing you have me managing your money so you don't make any foolish mistakes," Timothy said. "I'd hate to see you do anything you'd regret."

"What are you willing to do in life to be happy?" Angela asked. "Are you willing to do what it takes to please your clients?"

"I've always been a go-getter," Timothy answered.

"Hmm," Angela mumbled.

Timothy and Angela stayed at the restaurant another hour, having three more drinks each. After that Angela said, "I'll have my limo driver take us home. You can't drive like this," and then she laughed.

Timothy laughed and said, "I think you're right. I can barely make it to the door." They both walked out to Angela's limousine giggling all the way. They joked and laughed all the way to Angela's Park Avenue penthouse. When they got there, Angela said, "Come on up for a nightcap. My driver will take you home after that."

"Don't do it," Alexander mumbled under his breath.

"I guess it wouldn't hurt if I came up for a drink," Timothy said. "After all I am your financial advisor." They both laughed, and went up to Angela's high rise apartment. When they got inside, Timothy couldn't believe how luxurious it was. The living room was almost as big as his entire loft. He saw marble flooring and exquisite murals that must have cost a fortune. Expensive artwork hung on every wall; handcrafted vases adorned the tables. The place looked like a palace, with Angela as the residing queen.

Angela put some music on and poured Timothy and herself a strong drink. Angela tossed hers down, turned to Timothy and said, "I'm one up on you."

Timothy gulped down his drink and Angela poured them each another. Before he could finish it, Angela tossed hers down again. "Slow down," said Timothy, "I'm going to be one behind you all night."

Two drinks later Angela turned to Timothy, kissed him and said, "I've been attracted to you since the moment I saw you."

Timothy looked into Angela's beautiful eyes, and at her beautiful body, and was totally aroused. He was beyond drunk, and didn't think twice about resisting her.

When Timothy woke up the next morning with the worst headache he'd ever had, it took him a moment to realize where he was. He jumped out of bed, knowing he had made the worst mistake of his life.

"I can barely watch," Alexander said. "I don't think I like him anymore."

"You haven't seen anything yet," Andrew said. "You know when a man does things like that, the lies have to follow as he tries to cover up his wrongdoings. It's usually worse than if he just owned up to what he did."

"It's a shame Angela came into his life," Alexander said. "Maybe this wouldn't have happened."

"Don't forget how devious the other side is," Andrew said. "They probably sent Angela into Timothy's life just to ruin it. He still had the free will to say no, and he didn't. The consequences are going to be severe and now he's going to have to live with them."

They watched Timothy head home to face Frances. When he walked in, she said, "Where have you been? I've been worried sick."

Timothy knew he was in deep trouble and tried to cover up what he did by lying. "I had too much to drink and couldn't drive home so I grabbed a hotel for the night."

Frances, now crying, said, "And you couldn't even call me and tell me where you were."

Timothy started to think of yet another lie, but Frances cut him off. "Don't even bother. I was on the phone all night and found out you spent the night at Angela Farnsworth's apartment. I can smell her perfume on you from here. Her people weren't discreet at all about it. She's really arrogant to not even have her people deny it. I hope you're happy. How could you?" She ran into the bedroom locked the door and yelled, "We're through. Get out of here and don't come back."

Ryan and Ashley stumbled sleepily into the room and looked at their father and the closed door. Ryan cried out, "Mommy! Are you all right?"

Frances opened the door and gathered her children into her arms, saying, "Everything's going to be all right." She turned to Timothy and shouted, "How could you? Get out! And don't come back!"

Timothy gathered a few things and had nowhere to go so he went right to work on a Saturday, overwhelmed with guilt. He could not believe he had broken his wedding vows and cheated on his wife. He sat in his car for over a half an hour crying, then went into his office.

That night, he went home and tried to make up with Frances. "I'm so sorry for what I did. I will never do anything like that again. Will you forgive me?"

Frances had cooled off a little by then, but her face was still serious, "I forgive you for what you did, but I will never take you back. Our marriage was over a long time ago when you decided your business was more important than me and the kids. It's over between us. I want you to move out."

"Please give me another chance," Timothy said. "I'll make it up to you."

"You'll make it up to me? What will you do, buy me another car? No, I don't think you'll ever understand how to make it up to me."

"I love you," Timothy said. "Please give me another chance."

"I can't go through this anymore," Frances said. "The only regret I have is that Ryan and Ashley are going to grow up without a father, but I guess they were doing that anyway. I'm filing for divorce, so pack up your things."

Frances took Ryan and Ashley and locked herself in Ashley's room and said through the door, "Take whatever you want. Just get out." Timothy packed up some of his things and went to a hotel temporarily until he could find a place to stay.

On Monday Frances met with a divorce attorney. Timothy went to the office and tried to focus on work, but couldn't. He was consumed by guilt; he felt that not only had he cheated on his wife, but he had cheated on his children as well. That afternoon Angela Farnsworth called. "Timothy, dear, I was wondering if you want to go out again tonight. I had a great time the other night and I'd like to pick up right where we left off."

Timothy knew it was over between him and his wife and was tempted to say yes. He thought for a moment, and said, "You know I'm a married man. My wife found out about us and she's probably going to file for divorce. I really can't go out with you anymore."

Angela said, "If she's filing for divorce, that's all the more reason why we should go out tonight. Let's celebrate! It's my birthday next week and we can do up the town. I know a place we can go where we can have a great time."

"I really can't,' Timothy said.

"I'm used to getting what I want, Timothy. I'll meet you at seven over at Ginetti's on Park Avenue. After that, my driver can take us anywhere we want to go."

"I'm sorry, Angela, I can't."

"Do I need to remind you that you are my financial advisor? I have an account with your firm for over three million dollars in it, love."

"I know how much money you have invested with us," Timothy said. "I want to keep our relationship professional."

"I see," Angela said. "Well, I'll see you tomorrow, perhaps."

"All right," Timothy agreed, and hung up.

"Well, at least he did the right thing there," said Alexander.

"Too little, too late," Andrew said. "The damage was done. Angela would've ended up dumping him anyway in a couple of weeks just as she's done with every other man she's been with. After she gets bored, she moves on to the next man and uses him just as she did Timothy."

Sure enough, the next day Angela withdrew all of her money from Timothy's business. For the first time in Timothy's life he was glad he lost a client, and he was sure he didn't want her back. He knew he could never make up for what he did to Frances, but he wanted to try.

For the next few months, Timothy refrained from dating other women while he tried to convince Frances to take him back. She refused; Timothy eventually dated a woman named Cara briefly before breaking it off. He was heartbroken about losing his wife, but realized there wasn't much he could do to take back the past.

Six months later at the divorce proceedings, he turned to his lawyer John Jacobs and said, "I hired you for a reason, you know. I don't want her to get anything if I can help it."

Jacobs said, "I can't guarantee anything. I hate to tell you this, but she's probably going to get at least half of everything you have."

"If she gets half of everything it'll hurt my business and set me back. My firm can't survive if I have to keep paying out that type of money."

"I understand your concern," said Jacobs. "You have to understand the judge is going to look at it as her owning half of everything. She is still going to have to raise your children. That's expensive."

"I know; I just don't want to lose everything I've worked for."

"Let's just see what the judge says and go from there."

The divorce went just as expected; Frances ended up getting half of everything, including his business. Timothy was so angry that on the way out of the courthouse he couldn't control himself and told Frances, "I hope you're happy. Now you can live in luxury while I have to struggle. You didn't work for that money. It's not fair."

"Not fair?" Frances shot back. "It's not fair that my children don't have a father to speak of. It's not fair that they'll think of you as a cheat. I'm sure one day they'll find out what happened even if I try to keep it a secret. You know they won't be young forever. And besides, how much do you need? You have plenty of money left to survive."

"Survive," snarled Timothy. "I shouldn't have to barely survive after all I've done for you. You can take my money and blow it, for all I care. On second thought, I just might not pay you at all."

"I'm sure you'd do that to your children," Frances said. "What's next, Timothy? Are you going to pick a fight with me because you lost? You don't get it, do you? It's not about the money. You'll never understand that. Leave me alone and let me know when you're coming for visitation. We have to set up a schedule. That's if you have any precious time to spare."

Timothy gave her a dirty look and walked away; he spent the rest of the day sulking in his new apartment. The next day he went to the office and started working harder than ever to secure more clients, wanting to make up for what he was going to have to pay out.

A month later, Timothy made another insider trade that netted his firm a sizable amount of money. He was right back where he had started, slaving for the almighty dollar again, but this time as a single man. That trade alone enabled him to pay Frances and keep control of his business.

Timothy met a woman three months later and started dating her steadily. She was a woman that cared a lot about money and how she looked in society, so she and he got along well in the beginning.

Timothy exercised his visitation rights at first and then slowly phased them out. Instead of seeing his children every other weekend after a few months, he started seeing them once a month. Timothy's new girlfriend was increasingly demanding of his time and Timothy chose to see her instead on the weekends. Frances was badly hurt by this but figured that it would be that way eventually.

"His life is a mess," said Alexander.
"It gets much worse," said Andrew.
"How could it get any worse?"
"Just wait and see."

Frances couldn't stand living in the city any longer. The divorce, coupled with the fact that Timothy was showing less and less interest in seeing Ryan and Ashley, prompted her to move back to upstate New York. It was an hour and a half drive from the city. Frances made an agreement with Timothy that if he wanted to exercise his visitation rights, she would meet him halfway. This worked for a little while, until Timothy stopped calling Frances to meet her.

Timothy and his girlfriend broke up a little while later, and Timothy was alone once again. After that, he exercised his visitation rights a few times; seeing Ryan and Ashley became an every other month ordeal for him, which didn't surprise Frances.

A little over a year after the divorce, Timothy started drinking more and more. He also experimented with more prescription drugs, and his business began to suffer. The few times Timothy did pick up his children for the weekend, he drank when they went out and of course Ryan and Ashley told Frances about it.

She became concerned, and when Timothy called to pick up the children the next time she said, "I've heard that you're drinking quite a bit when you take Ryan and Ashley.

Do you think you can wait until after you drop them off until you drink? I don't want them around you when you've been drinking. Whatever you believe, I want them to have good memories of you. They love you and I don't want them to see you as a lush."

Timothy flew off the handle. "There you go again, trying to tell me what to do. Didn't you have enough of that when we were married? If you've ever looked at our divorce certificate you'd see that you're not married to me anymore. I drink a little. So what?"

"I don't think it's a good idea around the children," Frances said.

"You don't think anything is a good idea," Timothy said. "Maybe I shouldn't come anymore to see Ryan and Ashley. How would you like that?"

Frances knew Timothy was trying to use the children to get her back and to get his own way. She thought for a moment and said, "Maybe you're right. If you're going to be drinking so much, it might not be a good idea for you to see Ryan and Ashley."

"Well maybe I won't," Timothy said angrily, and hung up. He didn't pick up Ryan or Ashley that weekend.

"I'm very disturbed," Alexander said.

"As long as man has been around he never learns," Andrew said. "Despite what history shows them over and over again, man still chases after the wrong things in life like money and fame. It seems mankind will never understand that when you live a simple life, you live a happy life. All that stress and worry is bad for a man's health and soul. When he resorts to alcohol and drugs instead of facing his problems head on, you know he's on the path of destruction. Timothy is no different. Watch."

A couple of months later, Timothy was pulled over in a routine traffic stop. The police officer asked, "Can you get out of the car, please?"

Timothy asked, "Do you know who I am?"

"Yes I know who you are sir," the officer said. "I'm holding your driver's license."

"I own a very successful investment firm," Timothy slurred.

"Please step out of the car," the officer said again.

Timothy stumbled a little getting out of the car. The officer said, "I want you to put your feet together and walk a straight line."

Timothy swayed with every step he took. Next the officer gave Timothy a breathalyzer device and said, "Blow into this."

Timothy struggled to hold it and finally blew into it. The officer looked at the results and said, "Sir, you are way over the legal limit for alcohol. You're under arrest."

Timothy was taken to jail and charged with drunk driving. He was arraigned and released on bond the next morning. He showed up for work late and missed a very important meeting. His client took that as a sign that he wasn't serious about his business, and refused to reschedule. He lost a big client that day for the first time because of his own inadequacies.

Timothy was beside himself, and tried to rationalize his failure as a simple mistake and figured he couldn't win that client over anyway.

"I don't like the path he's taking," Alexander said

"When everything is going well people don't think twice about life," Andrew said. "When their back is up against the wall and things are falling apart is when you see a man's true character. It gets much worse, you'll see."

Timothy tried to get another insider deal, which didn't go through. The economy took a terrible downturn and stock market averages fell considerably. Commodity prices fell too. Unlike before, when everything Timothy touched seemed to turn into a profit, now everything he did seemed to turn into a loss.

Despite his advice, many of his clients closed their accounts and took a cash position to weather the economic storm that they felt was surely coming. Nearly thirty percent of Timothy's business vanished in six weeks. Timothy tried to hold on and pumped in more and more of the money he had made over the years to try to keep the firm afloat.

It worked for a while, but Timothy's business was slowly running out of money. He had stashed a good portion of personal cash away from his business, promising himself he would never touch it even in case of an emergency. He still didn't touch it now, and looked for other options to help his company survive.

"This is where you're going to go down and try to help recover his soul," Andrew said. "You're going to enter his life at this point where he's almost hit rock bottom. You'll dress normally, as a living person. This way, if he does believe in you, it's of his own faith. We'll wait until Phillip comes back and lets us know who the other side is sending, and then you'll be given your instructions. You can go now, Alexander, and I'll call for you before you leave. You're dismissed."

Meanwhile, the other side was wasting no time at all, in a level of hell where the only light came from the never-ending fire that burned and scorched the devils that didn't follow explicit orders. Nonstop screams and wails from continuous pain bolted through the air. A loud noise similar to the sound of a kettle drum thundered, and a booming voice from the depths of hell said, "George Samuels, report immediately."

The voice belonged to one Quinn Archibald, who had been a soldier in the English army in the thirteenth century. He was an evil man, without a compassionate bone in his body, who had exercised terror on his enemies whenever he could. Archibald had used his authority as a commander to institute some of the most heinous crimes of his era and was responsible for the slaughter of many innocent women and children. Now poor George Samuels hastened to report to him.

"Samuels," Archibald said. "A man named Timothy Fletcher is almost ours. He's the usual type, with a love of money, status, power, and women. You know the scenario."

George Samuels had been an executioner during the seventeenth century. He had enjoyed his work during his life, as merciless as any man that had walked the face of the earth. He knew all the dirty tricks to steal a man's soul in the blink of an eye. He welcomed all challenges to return to earth to wreak havoc on any soul he could.

"I want you to review Timothy Fletcher's life and his ex-wife's. Go down and try to steal both their souls at the same time," said Archibald. "Frances Fletcher is her name; his children are Ryan and Ashley. If you get Fletcher's ex-wife's soul, you'll have his too. Then we'll surely be able to get the brats' souls when they grow up. Foster resentment and anger towards Timothy in his wife and kids until they can't control themselves anymore. They have to hate what he's done to them and reach the point where they won't forgive him."

"I know what to do," Samuels said.

"I know you do," Archibald said. "This one isn't going to be as easy as you think. She's a former school teacher and loves children more than anything. You know how I hate that type. She has a pure heart and a strong will. It's going to take a lot to break her."

"Oh, I'll break her," Samuels said.

"Don't underestimate this one," Archibald said. "She has a faith that you're going to have to destroy. Her one weakness could be her deep love for her children. She's in much pain and resents that her children have to grow up without a father. What a fool. Maybe you can use that against her in some way. After we get her soul, I'll make sure she's tortured for two hundred years before I give her a chance like the one I've given you, to return to earth as a soul-stealer."

"Who are they sending down to fight for her?" Samuels asked.

"An angel named Alexander Hargrove," Archibald said. "I don't know much about him except he lost his last three souls and hasn't been down in quite a while."

Samuels laughed evilly and said, "Hargrove. Are you kidding me? They must be desperate if they're sending him. I worked on a soul against him before and had it converted in a week. He hardly put up a fair fight for that wretched man's eternal damnation."

Archibald raised his voice and warned, "Don't get over-confident on this one. Frances Fletcher hasn't lost her faith yet and it's going to take a lot to make her do so. If anyone can do it, I'm sure it's you. Remember, there could be four souls involved if you convert her."

"I'll get her," Samuels said with a wicked look in his eyes. "You wait and see. I love bringing the tough ones down to their knees and making them beg for help. They're so weak in times of trouble. It's pathetic."

"Start reviewing their lives right away," Archibald said. "I have word they're sending Hargrove down immediately."

"I'll get on it at once," Samuels said with a smile, and he did so.

Andrew called for Alexander to return and said, "I just received word that the other side is sending one of their toughest converters right away on this one – George Samuels."

"Samuels?" Alexander said. "Not twenty-six-in-a-row Samuels?"

"Twenty-seven," Andrew said. "He got back from an assignment early and converted the man in record time."

"Are you sure you want to send me?" Alexander asked. "Maybe you should send a more seasoned angel."

"I said before, we don't have anyone else, and time is running out," Andrew said. "Besides, do you know what it would look like for you if you stopped his streak? It would go a long way for you around here. Anyway, you haven't been down in so long that you have to go. You can beat him! I know you can!"

"I'll do the best I can," Alexander said. "It's just... I don't like Samuels."

"None of us do, Alexander. He's been a thorn in our side, if you pardon my expression, for over four hundred years. I'll tell you what I'll do. I'll let you go down and show yourself to Timothy. I know we don't do it often, but this time I'm going to allow it to give you an edge. Just think, you won't have to manipulate people's thoughts as much and send people in and out of his life all the time. You can do it all yourself because he'll be the only one that can see or hear you. That will help a lot."

"It will help," Alexander agreed.

"The only problem is that Samuels will be able to show himself to one person too," Andrew said. "You know how it works."

"Do you think it will be enough?" Alexander asked. "His wrongdoings are great and he seems very far from the right path. I've seen many men cast down for much less than what he's done."

"I know," Andrew said. "The list of his wrongdoings is long. It's not our place to decide who gets another chance, and you know that. I'm sure this will be the very last opportunity to save him, so make the most of it. Bring him back to us and don't let Samuels intimidate you. Timothy won't be able to see Samuels anyway; he'll just be able to see you. You know he's going to throw everything he can at him, wealth, power, false promises, and probably women. He'll try to exploit all Timothy's weaknesses at every chance possible. And with him in this vulnerable state, he's going to need everything you have. Now go. I'll be watching over you."

Alexander got ready to go back to earth. He was worried about what to do and how to handle the situation. As he left, he thought, *I can't stand Samuels. He's so cocky and con-fident. He uses every dirty trick in the book. I hope I can save Timothy — for his sake and mine.*

part two

the fight on earth

ᴄᴋ 7 ᴅᴏ

Timothy's life had unraveled more than ever before. His firm was struggling terribly and his investors weren't happy that their accounts weren't making money. Timothy was genuinely worried about his future and being able to pay his child support to Frances.

He decided it would be a good idea to take the edge off, go out to the bar and have a few drinks. It was during his fifth drink that Samuels arrived on earth, just before Alexander did. Samuels figured if he could get Timothy's soul right away then his job with Frances, Ryan and Ashley would be that much easier.

Samuels decided to stay with Timothy the entire night, thinking it would be best if he tried temptation right away to steal his soul before Alexander appeared. Samuels was confident that he might be able to persuade Timothy to do something stupid, maybe even take his own life.

Samuels had seen many cases where an ex-wife had made her former husband miserable to the point he wanted to give up. He had watched ex-husbands feel their former spouses' scorn like a knife turning in their stomach. Resentment and jealousy were powerful and favorite tools of his, and this time would be no different. Since Timothy was inebriated, Samuels immediately sent a strange woman over to him to tempt him to take her home. When she walked up she said, "You look like you could use a friend."

At first Timothy didn't pay much attention to her. Finally he said, "It's been a rough year for me, with the economy and all."

"It's been a rough year for everyone," the woman said. "My name's Sarah. I'm pleased to meet you."

"I'm Timothy Fletcher. Can I buy you a drink?"

"Absolutely," Sarah said. "I haven't seen you around much. Do you come here often?"

"I've never been here," said Timothy. "I don't know why I came in. I guess I just wanted to go somewhere different to forget about my problems for a while."

The two of them talked for an hour, until Sarah said, "Do you want to come over to my place? I only live about a mile from here."

Timothy was tempted, but for some odd reason he said, "No. I just want to be alone tonight."

Samuels was surprised that Timothy didn't take her right there from what he'd seen of Timothy's life. He put tempting thoughts in Sarah's head. Sarah turned to Timothy and pulled her blouse down a little so Timothy could see more cleavage. She said again, "Are you sure you don't want to come over? It'll be fun."

Timothy stared at her blouse, and gulped. "I don't think so. I don't feel like it tonight. I don't know what's wrong with me."

"Come on over and you can forget about everything for a while," Sarah said. "I'll make sure of that."

"No," Timothy said. "I just want to be alone right now. I have too much to think about."

"Hmm. You don't know what you're missing," Sarah said, and walked away.

About an hour after that, Timothy went home. He pulled out a bottle of vodka from the cupboard and poured himself another drink.

Samuels watched as he sipped it. He put a suggestion into Timothy's mind: *Go get the sleeping pills out of the medicine cabinet. It wouldn't hurt to take one. It'll help you sleep and forget about your problems for a while.*

With the bottle of vodka in his hand, Timothy went into the bathroom and grabbed a bottle of the strongest pills he had. He opened the bottle and looked at them. *All you have to do is take five of these, have another drink, and all your troubles will be over. You won't feel a thing and you won't ever have to worry about anything again. Just take them right now and everything will be all right.*

Timothy looked in the mirror and couldn't stand what he saw: a drunken fool, helpless in life. His wife was gone; his money was almost gone and he couldn't stand what he had become. He picked up the bottle of pills and poured five of them into his hand. He looked back in the mirror and heard a voice inside his head say: *Go ahead. You won't feel a thing.*

He brought his hand to his mouth and was just about to take the pills when a vision of Ashley flashed through his head. Another voice inside him said: *Don't do it. She needs you.*

He opened his hand and began to tremble, dropping the pills into the sink as he continued to look at his sorry reflection. He clenched the bottle of vodka in his fist, then dropped it in the sink, where it broke. He started to pick up the glass and cut himself on his palm and thumb. He threw the glass at the mirror and yelled, "No! I can't do it, no!"

He grabbed a towel, wrapped his hand, and fell to his knees and then to the ground, crying, "I can't, I just can't." He passed out on the floor next to the toilet.

Samuels watched and thought, *I almost had him. He's weak, really weak. It was worth an early try to get to him first. I wish I could've gotten him before Hargrove comes down. That would've showed them. Hargrove's power is going to be strong, but he's too stupid to know how to use it. I'll get you Fletcher, you wait and see, and I'll get your ex-wife and kids while I'm at it. And when you get to hell, I'm going to make sure you're tortured beyond belief.*

The next morning Timothy woke up on the bathroom floor and realized what he'd almost done. He felt sick to his stomach and had yet another headache. He took a couple of Motrin, made his way to the kitchen and dressed his cuts, which were not that severe. He got ready for work not knowing that today would be one of the most unusual days of his life.

At his office, Timothy turned on the computer and started surfing the upcoming events of the day to see if there were any good buys. He had become an expert at knowing the difference between a great investment and a losing prospect. The problem was that with the downturn in the economy, almost all his prospects lately were losing ones.

After a few minutes, Timothy's phone rang. His assistant Karen said, "Mr. Fletcher, it's Josh Bandy on the line. He says it's really important."

"Put him through," said Timothy, then he answered, "Hey, Josh. How are things going?"

"As well as can be. The economy is terrible and we've had some bad luck lately."

"*You've* had bad luck," Timothy said. "My investors are heading for the hills. They all see what's coming and want to maintain a cash position. You know what that does for us."

"You aren't kidding," Josh said. "The reason why I called is I got a big tip this time, right from the inside. A software company is going to be taken over by another firm. It's a huge deal and it's supposed to go down tomorrow. We're looking at twenty to thirty percent at least, overnight. The only problem is you're going to have to move on it right away. Like I said, it's going down tomorrow. Do you want in?"

"Yes I want in," Timothy said. "I need this one really bad."

"This one's going to cost you thirty thousand and the money has to be transferred by the end of the day," Josh said. "It's a big one though. When I tell you who it is, you won't believe it."

"I'm in," Timothy said. "The money will be in the account today."

"I trust you on this one buddy," Josh said. "Just make sure you transfer it before five."

"I will."

"The company's name is Dataware," Josh said. "It's a sure thing."

"Dataware!" Timothy said. "Are you sure?"

"Yes I'm sure. I couldn't believe it either when I heard. Who would've thought they'd get hit with a hostile takeover?" Josh paused and said, "Hey, it's not our place to decide what happens in business. It's our job to make sure our clients make money, and that's what we're doing. There's nothing wrong with that."

"You're right about that," Timothy said.

"I have to go," Josh said. "I'm buying Dataware right when the market opens. Don't forget. Have the money in the account by five o'clock."

"Will do, buddy," Timothy said, "and thanks." Then he hung up and called Randy. "How much do we have in liquid assets for trading?"

Randy looked at his computer. "We only have about six million left."

"All right, thanks. I'm making a huge trade today when the market opens with most of it."

"Are you sure that's wise?" Randy asked. "You know how you're not supposed to put all your eggs in one basket."

"Josh called me this morning," Timothy said.

"I see," Randy said. "That's awesome. I got a feeling we're going to be back on top after this."

"I hope so," Timothy said. "That's almost everything we have. If it doesn't work out, we'll probably be bankrupt."

Both Timothy and Randy paused and sighed. Timothy said, "I didn't get to where I am today without taking risks. I'm doing it. I don't care. I can't live like this anymore always worrying about whether we're going to make it another month with this economy."

"I've always trusted your judgment before, boss," Randy said. "There's no reason why I shouldn't trust it now."

"I'm doing it," Timothy said.

"Go for it, boss."

Timothy hung up and got everything ready to make the trade. All he had to do was push a button when trading started.

Five minutes before the market opened, Timothy sat at his desk nervously knowing that if he did this and it didn't work out, he'd be ruined. There would probably be an investigation and he'd probably be brought up on charges. His business would be in complete disarray and bankruptcy would be his only choice. His kids would have to go without for the first time in their lives and Timothy's license to trade would probably be suspended indefinitely.

His heart started beating faster and faster as the seconds passed until the market opened. A bead of sweat rolled down his forehead and his hands shook as he watched the final countdown before trading started. He had never been this desperate in his life and he hated it. It was success or failure and he knew he had no choice but to go through with it.

Suddenly, Alexander appeared, standing before Timothy's desk. He was dressed in dark pants and a sports coat, and looked down at his attire as if he was not used to wearing such clothes.

Timothy did a double take and gasped as Alexander said, "Don't do it. You'll be sorry."

Timothy hesitated and stuttered a little and said, "Don't... what? Who are you? How'd you get in here?"

"I just popped in," Alexander said.

Timothy picked up the phone. "Karen, get security up here right away."

"You shouldn't make that trade," Alexander said as Timothy hung up.

"What do you know about this trade?" Timothy asked. "Do you know Josh?"

"Oh, I know Josh well," Alexander said.

"Did he send you here to tell me not to go through with it?" Timothy asked.

Alexander laughed for a long moment and said, "No he didn't send me here. The one who sent me is much more important and powerful than Josh Bandy."

"If it wasn't Josh then why would you tell me not to do it and how do you know about it anyway?" Timothy asked. "Only a few people in the world know about this. It's a sure money maker."

"Oh, it's a sure money maker," Alexander said. "The only problem is it's illegal and you know it."

"Little man, get out of here and don't ever come back," Timothy said. "I know what I'm doing. I'll have you arrested for breaking and entering. Who do you think you are?"

"My name is Alexander Hargrove and I'm here to help you."

"I don't need your help!" Timothy yelled. "Now get out of here! The market is about to open."

A security guard knocked on the door and entered. Timothy looked at the countdown –there were only a few seconds left until the opening bell. The security guard said, "Yes sir, what can I do for you?"

"You can get this idiot out of here because I'm very busy," Timothy said, and he looked up from his computer.

Alexander was gone! Timothy looked all around and shook his head in bewilderment.

The security guard asked, "What idiot, sir?"

Timothy hesitated, looked around again and shook his head. "He must have left because he knew you were coming. He probably got scared just like all kooks do when they're threatened with arrest. You can go now, and if I need you again I'll call you."

The security guard left and Timothy looked at the screen on his computer. He noticed that trading had started and he nervously put his finger over the button to make the trade. With a deep breath, he pushed the button which executed the transaction. Then he took another deep breath and sat and stared into space for a couple of minutes. He knew what he had done was going to determine his entire future and all he could do now was wait and hope.

Josh is usually accurate, he thought. *His information has to be right, it has to.*

Timothy was on pins and needles over the next few hours until Alexander came to him again. Alexander was standing in front of his desk and said, "Worried about what you did? I would be too, if I were you."

"I can't believe you're back. Get out of here or I'll call security again."

"It won't matter if you do," Alexander said. "They can't do anything to me."

Timothy picked up the phone again. "Karen, send security up here right away and watch my door this time to see if anyone leaves so you can let security know where they went."

"Yes, sir," said Karen.

Timothy turned back to Alexander. "What do you want and what are you doing here?"

Alexander smiled and said, "I'm here to help you."

Timothy raised his eyebrows. "The only way you can help me is if you open an account with us or give me a stock tip like the one I just got. Can you do either of those things?"

Alexander laughed loudly. "Open an account or give you a stock tip. That's funny."

Timothy said, "You have three seconds to get out of here or I'm going to have security escort you out and arrest you. Do you understand?"

Alexander laughed again and said, "You can't hurt me. I'm not from here."

"I don't care where you're from. We have laws here in this state and you're trespassing. I'll prosecute you to the fullest extent of the law if you don't leave right now."

Alexander said, "I'm going to leave right now, to give you some time to think about what you did today. I'll see you again very soon."

There was a knock at the door and a voice behind it that said, "Did you call for security?" Timothy opened it; the security guard was standing there ready to take action.

Timothy looked at the security guard and said, "Get this guy out of here and have him arrested. I want him brought up on trespassing charges." He turned to Alexander, and once again there was no one there.

The security guard looked around and asked, "Have who arrested, sir?"

Timothy shook his head again in disbelief. "Never mind. He must have left."

"Are you all right, Mr. Fletcher? That's the second time you called us today."

"I'm fine," Timothy said. "I don't know what's going on. Forget about it. You can go."

After the security guard left, Timothy walked out to Karen's desk and asked, "Did you see anyone pass here besides the security guard?"

Karen shook her head and said, "No, sir."

"Are you sure?" Timothy asked.

"I'm absolutely sure, sir."

Timothy walked back into his office, confused, and sat down to survey the early figures from Wall Street. There was no news yet about Dataware so he spent the afternoon worrying.

The next morning as the stock market opened Timothy watched nervously. He waited and waited until shortly before lunch. Just before noon, a company called Disk Unlimited, announced an offer to buy out Dataware. They offered four dollars a share higher than the price of the stock. The stock went through the roof after that and increased seven dollars a share from what Timothy had paid.

Timothy quickly placed an order to sell the entire lot. His company made nearly a million and a half dollars in just one day. Timothy was relieved and excited until Randy came to him and said, "That was a great trade you made today. I'm a little concerned, though, that people might ask some questions about it. You know whenever you make a trade like that it opens people's eyes. I don't want to take too many risks and take a chance of getting caught."

"Let me handle it," Timothy said. "I'm the boss, aren't I? I'm not worried about it and you shouldn't be either. We didn't do anything wrong."

"Maybe you're right," Randy said.

"I'm always right, aren't I?" Timothy gloated.

Randy left and Alexander appeared. "I'll bet you feel horrible right now, don't you?" Alexander asked.

"It's you again, little man," Timothy said. "I thought I told you not to come back. I'm calling security again."

"It won't do any good, just like before."

"What do you want?" Timothy asked.

"Like I told you," Alexander said. "I'm here to help you."

"You're here to help me? If I'd listened to you I'd have lost a fortune. Apparently I should never listen to you. The next time you have a stock tip, keep it to yourself. You told me not to buy Dataware. It went through the roof. My company made a fortune."

Alexander shook his head and said, "You made a fortune illegally. You ought to be ashamed of yourself."

"Why am I even talking to you?" Timothy complained. He reached for the phone to call security; suddenly a company's name and stock symbol popped up on his screen. Timothy said, "What the," and stopped speaking to look at his computer more closely.

"Chemtrex," he murmured. "I've never heard of them."

Alexander thought, *Nice touch, Samuels. Giving him a stock tip is ingenious. You know how money-fixated he is and you're playing right into his weaknesses. I'll take care of that.* Alexander slightly snapped his fingers and the computer screen went blank.

Timothy picked up the phone, called Karen and said, "Get security up here right away." Then he called Randy and said, "Get me as much information as you can on a company called Chemtrex. It trades under the symbol CXX. I want balance sheets, price-to-earnings ratios, debt-to-cash ratios, and everything else you can find out about them. I even want to know if the stock boy on the loading dock has sneezed in the last six months. I mean everything you can find out. Do I make myself clear?"

"Yes sir," Randy said.

"And by the way, I want it on my desk in two hours," Timothy said.

"Two hours?" Randy said. "That's impossible."

"Have it here," Timothy said and hung up.

He turned back to Alexander and said, "I've had about enough of you. Get out of here and don't come back."

"I wouldn't buy that stock if I were you," Alexander said.

"And why's that? You were dead wrong about the last trade and you're probably wrong about this one."

"I wasn't wrong about the last trade and I'm not wrong about this one," said Alexander. "Nothing good can come from those trades."

"Nothing good can come from the trade I made yesterday? Are you joking? I made a fortune."

"It's not the amount you made," Alexander said. "It's how you made it. In the long run, money earned like that will do nothing but bring you sorrow."

"Are you crazy? Bring me nothing but sorrow? You're talking nonsense." Timothy paused and said, "For the last time who are you?"

Alexander sighed and said, "I'm your guardian angel."

Timothy looked at Alexander and laughed. "That's a good one." He laughed even harder than before and said, "You aren't an angel. You're a fool."

Alexander sighed. "I guess I'm not much of an angel yet, but I was all they had."

There was a knock at the door again and a voice that said, "Security."

Timothy walked to the door and said, "Just wait down the hall. Everything is fine."

The security guard said, "Yes, sir," and went down the hall.

"Let me get this straight," Timothy said. "You're saying you're my guardian angel and you're here to help me."

"That's right."

"You're kookier than I thought," Timothy laughed. "If you're my guardian angel, then I'm the president of the United States."

"Nice to meet you, Mr. President," Alexander said. "Would you like your coffee in the Oval Office?"

Timothy gritted his teeth and said, "You're insane! I'm going to see to it that you get a nice padded room over at the mental hospital." He headed for the door to get security, but Alexander asked, "Am I insane? Is it so crazy that it couldn't happen? I know everything about you."

Timothy stopped and asked, "Yeah like what?"

"I know when you were born and that you lived on a farm growing up in Wisconsin."

"Everyone knows that. Tell me something no one knows." Timothy paused and said, "Forget it. I can't believe I'm even having this conversation." Timothy edged towards the door to get the security guard again.

"I know you were married to a lovely woman named Frances and have two children named Ryan and Ashley. Ashley is adorable. You should really get up to see her more often."

Timothy's face turned red from the guilt he felt over being a lousy father and said, "You leave my family alone! Take this!"

Timothy swung wildly at Alexander, who disappeared, only to reappear on the other side of the room. "Violence never solves anything, Timothy."

Timothy, dazed and unsure of what had just happened, shook it off and said, "How did you do that and how do you know so much about me?"

"I told you. I'm your guardian angel. I was sent here to help you."

Timothy blinked at Alexander, not knowing what to think. "I know what this is. This is some kind of reality show or something that my friend Josh put you up to, to see how I react."

"This is no joke," Alexander said. "I'm here to save you and your family from eternal damnation."

Timothy laughed and said, "Come on out, Josh. I'm not falling for it."

"Josh Bandy is in Boston right now," Alexander said. "He has his own problems to deal with. In time Josh will fall to his knees begging for help, just as people like him always do."

"Come on. You don't expect me to believe this, do you?"

"You can believe what you want, Timothy, but it's true."

"Anyone could know where I was born," Timothy sneered. "That's an easy one. Tell me something only I would know."

"I know everything about you because I reviewed your life before I came here for my assignment."

"Get out of here, you nut. Your assignment! That's a good one. I don't believe you one bit."

"You mustn't keep telling me to leave or I might end up having to go for good and then you'll be written off as a lost soul. If I don't show some results soon, it could be all over for you."

"All right," Timothy said. "Where did I go to college?"

"The University of Wisconsin," Alexander said. "You went on a full-ride scholarship and hurt your arm in the last game of your junior year and could never pitch again."

Timothy looked at Alexander and said, "That was an easy one. What was my record in my junior year in high school?"

"You were fifteen and three and led the league in strike-outs," Alexander said. "You were unstoppable that year."

Timothy paused still in disbelief.

"I know everything about you," Alexander said. "I know about the pie you took when you seven years old and lied to your parents about it."

"I never took that pie!" Timothy shouted.

"Oh yes, you did," Alexander said. "I saw you. You threw the plate in the ditch hoping you wouldn't get caught."

Timothy, fuming with the built-up rage of his childhood, yelled, "Get out of here and don't come back! I don't know how you knew those things or what kind of tricks you're using. All I know is I want you out of here now."

He opened his office door, stepped out and called down the hall for security. When he and the security guard went back into his office, Alexander was gone. The security guard said, "What can I do for you sir?"

Timothy looked around and said, "Nothing. I'm fine. If I need you, I'll call."

The security guard said, "Are you sure you're all right sir? You look a little pale."

"I'm fine," Timothy said. "Just shut the door on the way out."

The security guard left and Timothy pulled a bottle of vodka out of his desk drawer and poured himself a drink. He took a long drink and thought, *I must be losing my mind. That weird man keeps coming and going as he pleases. Maybe I'm just seeing things. I really should make a doctor's appointment; I'm long overdue for a checkup. I'll have Karen make me one for next week.*

He picked up the phone and called Randy. "How long on that file for Chemtrex?"

"Sir, I don't understand," Randy said. "You just asked for it ten minutes ago. The Flash himself couldn't have gotten it to you that soon."

"Let me know the minute you get it."

"I will," Randy said.

Timothy poured himself another drink and waited for Randy to call. He sat there wondering again if he was seeing things or if the man who was pestering him was real.

An hour and a half later, Randy came in with the file on Chemtrex. Timothy asked, "Did you get a chance to review it?"

"A little," said Randy. Timothy grabbed the file and started looking at it. Randy began reading over his shoulder and said, "They're a drug company that researches new medicines. They had a major breakthrough about five years ago with a drug called Cerifex. It's used to treat high blood pressure. From what I saw it's very effective. They haven't come out with anything new lately and have been riding the coattails of that drug plus a few others they developed in the past. Their price-to-earnings ratio is very good. They have stability in the market and their debt-to-cash ratio is excellent. Chemtrex is listed on the NASDAQ and is trading for about fifteen dollars a share. It would be a solid buy for long term as far as a growth stock is concerned, but for short term, I don't know."

Timothy read carefully for several more minutes, reviewing every detail. After he was done he looked up with a confused look on his face and thought, *Why was that company's name on my computer screen and how did it get there?* Timothy said, "I think it's a buy."

"Do you want me to put a small order in?" Randy asked.

"No," Timothy said. "I'm going to put in a large order. I've got a feeling about this one. I'm going to transfer a million dollars from the money we made yesterday into Chemtrex. I can't explain why. I'm just going to do it."

"Sir, I hate to disagree with you, but unless you have some inside information that wouldn't be wise. Much of that money was from investors' accounts. All you made for the firm yesterday was a million. It's too much of a risk to put it all into a stock you're not sure about. I'm sorry sir, but that's what you pay me for, to make recommendations."

"I'm the head of this company," Timothy said "I say a million gets transferred into Chemtrex stock. I'll handle it personally."

"Yes, sir," Randy said.

Timothy set up the deal and just before the closing bell on Wall Street he hit the button to complete the purchase.

He went home that night and had a few more drinks, feeling pretty good about the money he had made in the last two days.

As he went to bed, he thought about the funny man he had seen, or thought he'd seen. He figured it was just his mind playing tricks on him. The last thing he thought before he dozed off was, *Guardian angel! Come on. There's no such thing, and anyway, I don't need any help.*

❦ 8 ❧

The next morning Timothy went to work like any other morning. He rummaged through the endless information that was supposed to help him make rational decisions about what stocks to buy and what stocks to sell. He went through a few accounts and checked their values. Then he checked a few of the hedge funds he and his clients were invested in.

He wasn't planning on making any major purchases for a while after how much he had made the day before. As the stock market opened he checked the value of Chemtrex and it hadn't changed. About an hour after trading started Randy burst into the office and said, "Did you hear the news?"

Timothy looked confused and said, "What news?"

"Chemtrex is on the morning business report." Randy rushed to turn on the TV and turned it to the correct channel. On the screen, the CEO of Chemtrex was speaking.

The host of the show said, "So what's the likelihood you'll have Aretel on the market before the end of the year?"

The CEO said, "Since the Food and Drug Administration gave us approval late yesterday, the chances are very good. We're going to start producing Aretel in large quantities within two months. It should be on the market in just over four months."

The host asked, "How effective is Aretel compared to the drugs out on the market in helping manage arthritis pain?"

The CEO grinned from ear to ear. "According to our tests, Aretel will be the most effective arthritis medication out there. It'll corner the market. We believe it's going to become one of the top-selling medications in the country. All our tests show Aretel has few or no side effects, which is rare for an arthritis medication."

"Congratulations," the commentator said. "There you have it, breaking news. Chemtrex gets FDA approval for Aretel. Chemtrex stock is up over seventy percent on the day so far. It's still early though. Thank you for joining us, Robert. That's Robert Cunningham, CEO of Chemtrex Incorporated. Good luck to you."

Randy turned off the TV and asked, "How did you know? Did you get a tip again from your source?"

Timothy paused. "I don't know how I knew, I just did."

"Wow," Randy said. "You told me to watch out for hunches and only to follow facts. If that wasn't a hunch, I don't know what was."

Timothy smiled and said, "Who cares how we did it? The fact is that we did it. Now let's watch this thing and wait for the perfect time to sell."

They watched the price of Chemtrex stock double and then drop back a little. By the end of the day it was up just over seventy-five percent. Timothy set up a sale and executed it just before the close of trading, liquidating every last share of Chemtrex he owned. He ended up with nearly seven hundred and fifty thousand dollars profit.

He went to Randy and said, "I can't believe it! We just had the two best single days in our company's history in bad economic times. No one can do that, no one."

"How does it feel to be rich?" Randy asked.

Timothy yelled enthusiastically, "It feels great! It's been one of the most trying times of my life and now we're back."

"Good job sir," Randy said.

"We need to go out and celebrate the greatest two days in our company's history," Timothy said. "Let's go out to the best restaurant in town. It's on me."

"I'd love to," Randy said. "I can't tonight though. I have to go to my son's hockey game. Tomorrow I can."

Timothy thought of his son and how he had bought him his first baseball glove, but never had many chances to use it with him. A feeling of emptiness washed over him, mixed with guilt from not seeing his son enough. He tried to satisfy himself by thinking about how much money he just made, but it didn't help.

He turned to Randy and said, "That's all right. I'm going to go out anyway." Randy smiled, and left for the day.

Timothy went home to his empty apartment and thought of Ryan and Ashley. He dialed Frances' number to see if he could see his children for the coming weekend. Frances didn't pick up, so he left a message. "It's me, Tim. I was just calling to see how you and the kids are. I was wondering if I could drive up this weekend and see them. Call me." His guilt lessened a little with the knowledge that he at least had made an effort.

He got ready and went out to an upscale bar with a wad of cash in his pocket. He normally never carried much cash on him and always used a credit card for all his purchases. This time it was a special occasion and he figured cash would be the appropriate thing to use.

He had a couple of drinks and bought rounds for several people. One of the women there spotted Timothy and sat down next to him. She was a regular there and chatted up wealthy single men on a normal basis.

"Hello," said Timothy. "Can I buy you a drink?"

She said, "Sure. My name's Lisa. What's yours?"

"I'm Tim, Tim Fletcher."

"Well Tim," Lisa said. "You look like you could use some company."

"Yeah, I'd like that." Timothy noticed Lisa's blonde hair and big blue eyes. She was expensively dressed, with a skin-tight blouse that showed off her cleavage. She was tall and slender and in beautiful shape.

"Are you married?" he asked her.

"No, and I don't have a boyfriend either."

"How is it that someone that looks like you doesn't have a husband or a boyfriend?"

"I had a husband, but not anymore."

Timothy pulled out the stack of cash and paid the bartender. Lisa, wide-eyed, said, "You shouldn't be walking around with a stack of bills like that. Don't you have a credit card or something?"

Timothy, who was starting to feel the effects of the drinks, slurred, "Yeah I have a credit card. I just had two of the best days of my life in a row and I wanted to make sure I had enough money to celebrate."

"You have plenty of cash for tonight. There must be ten grand there."

"Fifteen," Timothy said.

"You don't want to blow all that tonight, do you?"

"What does it matter? There's plenty more where that came from."

Lisa's attention was now totally fixed on Timothy. "What do you do for a living?"

"I'm a financial advisor," Timothy said. "I trade stocks and commodities or whatever else makes money."

"I see. What did you have planned for tonight?"

"I'm going to have a few more drinks and take the night step by step."

"Sounds good to me," Lisa said.

The two talked for two more hours and had a few more drinks. When it was time to leave, Timothy said, "Do you want to come to my place for a while? It's a really expensive apartment."

"Sure, I'll come over to your place," replied Lisa. They left in a cab and went up to Timothy's apartment. Even though Lisa knew he was wealthy by the way he dressed and acted, she couldn't believe how luxurious the apartment was. She hoped Timothy might be the one she'd been looking for her entire life.

After they talked and had another drink, Timothy slurred, "Do you want to go up to my bedroom?"

"Sure," said Lisa without hesitation. They went up to Timothy's bedroom and started kissing. As they moved over toward the bed, Timothy was startled by suddenly seeing Alexander over Lisa's shoulder. Alexander said, "Don't do it."

Timothy looked at him angrily and said, "Get out of here!"

"Excuse me?" said Lisa, surprised.

"I wasn't talking to you," Timothy said. "I was talking to him." Then he pointed at Alexander.

Lisa looked at where he was pointing, then back at Timothy and asked, "Who?"

"That little man that's been bothering me over there," Timothy said.

"Are you all right?" she asked. "I'll tell you what. You just lie down next to me on the bed and maybe you'll feel better."

"I feel fine," Timothy slurred. "It's just that man standing over there has been following me for days now."

"I'm telling you, I don't see any man," Lisa said. "Are you all right?"

"You mean to tell me you can't see that man over there?" Timothy asked, pointing to where Alexander was standing.

"No I don't see anyone."

"She can't see or hear me," Alexander said. "Only you can."

"Oh yeah," Timothy slurred. "You're my guardian angel. I forgot." He laughed wildly.

"You know what," said Lisa nervously, "I think I'd better be going. You can call me when you get it together. I think you'd better go to sleep for now."

"No, don't go," Timothy said. "I like you. Come here."

Lisa picked up her coat and said, "I'll get a cab. It's cool, don't worry about it." She walked out the door and didn't look back.

Timothy slurred, "Now look what you've done. I liked her."

"What you need right now is a good night's sleep," Alexander said. "The last thing you need is a woman like that."

"Like what?" Timothy asked.

"You don't need the kind of woman that only wants you for your money. If you get involved with a woman like that, your life will be more miserable than it is now."

"All right, Mr. Angel," Timothy laughed. "I'll lie down." The moment he did so, he passed out.

The next morning Timothy woke up with a splitting headache. He headed straight to the medicine cabinet and took three Motrin. *I had the weirdest dream last night,* he thought. *I'm glad that man is gone. I probably just dreamed I saw him for two days.*

He went to work as if nothing had happened. Alexander immediately appeared again and said, "You almost made a big mistake last night. You should be thanking me for saving you."

Timothy looked at Alexander and said, "I thought I was through with you. I'm going to ask you one more time: Who are you and why are you bothering me?"

"I keep telling you," Alexander said. "I'm your guardian angel and I'm here to help you."

"If you're here to help me, then why did you almost give me two bad stock tips in a row?" Timothy asked. "If I'd listened to you my company would still be on the verge of bankruptcy."

"Those tips you got were from the other side," Alexander answered. "Nothing good can come from them."

"Are you crazy? We had the two best days in our company's history and you say nothing good can come from it. And what's this all about when you say it came from the other side?"

"When I say the other side I mean down there." Alexander pointed toward the floor.

Timothy's eyes widened. "Are you seriously telling me you really are from heaven?"

"Absolutely," Alexander said. "The other side has somebody down here right now working to take the souls of Frances, Ryan and Ashley. If I can't convert you, they all could be lost."

"You're nuttier than a fruitcake."

"Am I?" Alexander asked. "Ask me anything you want about Frances, Ryan or Ashley."

"Okay. What's Ryan's favorite sport?"

"Soccer."

"Ah ha," said Timothy. "You're wrong. His favorite sport is baseball."

"No," Alexander disagreed. "You think his favorite sport is baseball, but it isn't. He plays soccer on a team now. He likes soccer much more than baseball."

"That's not right," Timothy said. "I know he loves baseball."

"Why?" Alexander asked. "Because you bought him his first baseball glove, that means he's supposed to love baseball? Oh yes, I saw you there at the sporting goods store when Ryan was three. The clerk's name was Justin if I'm not mistaken. You were never there to teach Ryan how to play baseball so he lost interest in it. Frances signed him up for soccer and you don't even know it. Do you know how pathetic you are?"

"Hey, little man, watch it," Timothy said. "Do you know who you're talking to?"

"By the way, I do have a name and it's Alexander Hargrove. I told you my name when we first met, and you showed me disrespect just because I'm short. And I do know who I'm talking to. I'm talking to Timothy Evan Fletcher, a greedy, dishonest, self-centered idiot who doesn't know what's important in life even though he's been given every sign imaginable to change."

"You better stop it," Timothy warned.

"Stop telling the truth?" Alexander said. "Why, does the truth hurt?"

"I'm a well-respected financial advisor," Timothy said. "I have the respect of my community."

Alexander laughed. "The respect of your community, that's a good one. You have the respect of people you make money for. Do you think if you were broke you'd have a friend in the entire world? Well, you wouldn't. They'd all throw you under the bus if it came to it. All the people you ever cared about, you turned your back on."

"Shut up!" Timothy yelled. "I've had enough!"

"You've had enough," Alexander said mockingly. "We've only just begun and poor Timmy Fletcher says he's had enough! Let me tell you, mister, this is your last chance and if you blow it, you're done."

Timothy couldn't control himself any longer. "No one talks to me like that! No one." He picked up a paperweight and threw it at Alexander, who of course vanished and reappeared.

Timothy was awakened to the fact that he couldn't do anything to Alexander. He thought for a moment and said, "All right. Let's suppose you are an angel and you were sent down to help me. Why me?"

"I've asked that myself a hundred times," Alexander said. "That decision was made by someone far superior to me; I just do as I'm told. I've seen many men cast down for much less than what you've done. Consider yourself lucky; if it weren't for your great-grandfather, your grandfather and your father's requests, I'm sure we would've given up on you a long time ago."

"My father," said Timothy spitefully. "Now, there was a well-to-do man. He slaved in the fields for years, and for what? So he could die of a heart attack and have his farm taken away just a few years after he died. I promised myself that I would never be like my father and I won't, no matter what you say."

Alexander frowned, looked up toward heaven and shook his head. "Are you no different than him? You slave over your business, worrying about losing it just like your father did the farm. I guess you two are a lot alike."

Timothy gritted his teeth and said angrily, "I'm not like him and never will be!"

"The first thing we need to do is get rid of that pent-up anger you have toward your father," Alexander said.

"Yeah, well, that's easier said than done."

"Talk about someone that's ungrateful," Alexander fired back. "You had the audacity to call Frances ungrateful when you mistreated her. Ha! No one is more ungrateful than you. Your father was ten times the man you'll ever be."

"My father—" Timothy began, but Alexander cut him off.

"Let me tell you a little about your father. Did you know that he saved your life when you were just a baby?" Timothy looked confused. "Oh, yes. When you were a mere child, you came down with the flu and your mother was pregnant with your brother and had it too. There had already been many deaths in the area from it. Your father stayed up with you for two nights in a row, applying cold compresses to your body trying to break the fever. He was exhausted, but never gave up. If it wasn't for him, you might not have made it. He paid a hefty price for that too. He lost a calf because of it and was set back weeks."

"You mean my father actually put me before his precious farm for once? That's hard to believe."

"Your father tried to teach you everything he could about the farm so you could have a good life like him," said Alexander, "but with your brother sick all the time, it was hard for him."

"My father did nothing but favor my brother and sister their entire lives," Timothy said. "He used me to get the work done around the farm while he let them do as they pleased."

"Your father was much harder on you than on Markus and Cindy. That's true," Alexander said. "The only reason why he had you work so hard was that he was trying to teach you to be a man. I guess you were too stubborn to understand that."

"My father loved both Markus and Cindy more than me. He always did things for them that he didn't do for me."

"Let me ask you something," Alexander said. "Do you treat Ryan and Ashley the same? I mean, Ashley is a girl, and she is much younger."

"Well no, I don't treat them the same."

"Exactly," Alexander said. "No parent is perfect. Let me ask you another question. If Ashley was sick with a condition like the one Markus had, would you expect her to do the same things Ryan did when she had to fight so hard to survive with her attacks?" Timothy thought for a second and Alexander said, "Well, would you?"

"No... I guess not," Timothy said.

"Then why did you expect your father to treat his own children any differently than you would? You were given the gift of health and intelligence, and all you could do is think of yourself and how you were treated unfairly. What if that had been you who had severe asthma? Would you have expected your father to turn his back on you and focus on your brother? Is that what he should've done?"

Timothy, at a loss for words, stared for a moment and then shouted, "Get out of here! I don't want your help! You heard me, get out of here!"

"If you keep saying that, I'm going to have to leave and I won't be back." Alexander looked deep into Timothy's eyes. "I'm going to give you a little time to think about your life. Remember that it was your father who convinced us to give you one more chance. He was a righteous man and he's up there right now, not down below. Don't give in to the other side. Your children are depending on you.

"Oh, and one other thing. I wouldn't take too long to decide, because a devil from the other side is organizing right now to get his claws into Frances and your children. He's very powerful and has been known to win over even the strongest people."

Alexander disappeared and Timothy was left with a blank look on his face. *This can't be happening. It's impossible. And what he said about my father, it can't be true. He has to be mistaken, he just has to be. What am I thinking? This isn't even real.*

As he cleared his mind, his phone rang. Samuels had no intention of letting Timothy question his life, and figured he'd tempt him with Timothy's strongest desire ever, money.

Timothy picked up the phone and Josh said, "Hey, buddy. I heard about your buy the other day. You could've let me know about Chemtrex."

"I wasn't sure about it," Timothy said. "It was just a hunch."

"Next time you get a hunch, let me know," said Josh. "I got another deal coming down. I have information about a company whose stock is going to shoot through the roof. They're on the verge of making an announcement about a breakthrough computer chip that's supposed to corner the market. This is a big one and it's going to cost fifty thousand. Are you in?"

Timothy hesitated this time and said, "Sure I'm in. I'll have the money in the account by the end of the day."

"The name of the company is Falco," Josh said. "Check them out. This one's going to make us a bundle."

"Thanks buddy," Timothy said and then he hung up.

Timothy set up the buy and executed it. After it was done, he felt a little guilty for the first time ever after an illegal deal. He wondered if what his so-called guardian angel said was true about his father. He wondered if he was crazy to even imagine that he had a guardian angel. He shook the thoughts from his head and went on with his day.

Later that evening, Timothy couldn't get the thought of Alexander and all that he had said out of his mind. He picked up the phone and thought, *I'm going to prove him wrong. I know my son better than anyone.* He dialed Frances' number and said, "Hi, Frances. This is Tim."

"Oh hi, how are you?"

"I'm all right, I guess," Timothy said. "How are the kids?"

"They're fine. You really should make a reasonable effort to see them more often. They miss you so much."

"I'll come up this weekend for sure," Timothy said.

"Yeah, I've heard that before," Frances countered.

"Don't start at me. Hey, is Ryan home?"

"He's here," Frances said.

"Can I talk to him?"

"Sure, I'll go get him."

Ryan came to the phone and his voice lit up with joy when he found out it was his dad. "Hi Daddy. When are you coming up to see us?"

"I'll try to make it up this weekend," Timothy answered. "Hey Ryan, I wanted to ask you something. How would you like to go get a new baseball mitt just like the one you got when you were little, but better?"

"Um, I guess," said Ryan. "I really don't play much baseball anymore. Daddy, I joined a soccer team and I love it! I have a bunch of friends on the team and we go places together like bowling and the movies and stuff. We have a really good team and I scored the winning goal last week. The whole team gave me high fives and we won the game four to three. I love it."

Timothy felt as though his heart had just dropped to the floor. He couldn't say anything. Ryan finally said, "Daddy, are you there?"

Timothy said, "I'm here, son."

Ryan said, "I have to go, Daddy. I have practice in an hour and I like to get there early and practice before everyone else gets there. Mommy loves to come to my practices and watch. Ashley does too. I have to go."

"I love you, son."

"I love you too, Daddy," Ryan returned. Then he hung up.

Timothy sat there with his mouth wide open. He couldn't believe how stupid he'd been. He couldn't believe what he'd been missing out on with his children all these years. Most of all, he couldn't believe that some so-called angel knew his son better than he did.

He put his head down on his desk and tried to rationalize his regret. *So what if Alexander was right? I'm going to focus on me and my business. We're doing great and I'm not giving that up. If he comes back I'm going to tell him off. Who does he think he is? A guardian angel – right, there's no such thing.*

The next day Randy came up to Timothy and said, "Business is booming! After everyone heard about those two awesome trades you made, it seems like everyone wants us to handle their investments. Four clients who had closed their accounts with us because of the downturn have called to reopen them. We have seven new prospective clients who will probably open accounts, and three more maybe's. I don't know how you did it, but you really turned things around."

"Hmm," said Timothy, under his breath.

"A couple of clients want to meet with you on Saturday," Randy said. "I told them you would. I know how you are about securing new money."

"This weekend? I can't. I have to go up to see my kids."

"Sir," said Randy anxiously, "Can't you go next weekend? These clients would provide huge accounts and increase our business tremendously. I can't cancel. We'd lose them for sure."

Timothy sighed and said, "All right. I'll keep the appointments, but don't book anything on Saturday for a while."

"I won't, sir," Randy said. "Yeah I thought it was sort of unusual that two people wanted to meet with you on the weekend."

Timothy mumbled, "Yeah, very unusual. I wonder."

"What did you say, sir?" Randy asked.

"Oh, nothing," Timothy said. "I've got some work to do, so I'll see you later."

Meanwhile, Samuels was finalizing his plan to secure Frances' and the children's souls. He had found the perfect person to manipulate into Frances' life: James Kruger, who had one foot in hell already. Six feet tall and extremely handsome, he was a womanizer of the worst kind, having learned over the years how to manipulate women, use them, and discard them like trash. He knew how to use his looks and demeanor to satisfy his unquenchable lust.

Samuels appeared to Kruger and openly told him who he was. Unlike his cautious counterpart Timothy, Kruger needed no convincing that he was being visited by a supernatural agent. It flattered his immense ego to see himself as important enough to be contacted by an agent of hell. Far from being intimidated by Samuels, Kruger was impressed by his boldness, relishing the chance for an adventure that few mortals could hope to carry off.

Samuels said, "I have a special commission to offer you. I want you to meet a woman named Frances Fletcher. She was married at one time and has two children."

"Two children?" Kruger said. "Ugh."

"Listen to me carefully," Samuels said. "I want you to go into her life and try to get her to fall in love with you. If you can get her to do this, we can bring her down just as I've planned. You'll need to ask her to marry you."

"Ask her to marry me?" Kruger said. "Are you crazy? I have three or four women that I'm seeing right now."

"Her one weakness," said Samuels, "is that she loves her children more than anything. She longs and prays for a man to raise her children with her. If you can convince her to marry you, then we can destroy her from within. The only way to do this is to convince her that you're the one to be a good father to her children. Convince her that you love all children, not just hers."

Kruger groaned. "No way! I hate kids."

"You can put up with them for a little while at least," Samuels said. "I would just tempt her with money but she doesn't seem to care about that."

"I won't do it," Kruger said. "I thought you were going to give me something fun to do. You want me to get married? I don't think so."

Samuels face turned as red as the hellfire he came from. He glared at Kruger and said, "You *will* do this and you *will* get married! You don't want to cross me! Do I make myself clear?"

Kruger, always arrogant, replied, "You don't scare me one bit. What I want to know is, what's in it for me?"

Samuels smiled to himself; he now knew he had chosen exactly the right person for the job. Aloud, he said, "Frances is quite a looker. And think about how you'll feel, knowing you're the one that sent her to the other side. Don't you welcome the challenge? Why stop at a woman's body, or even her heart, when now you can even take her soul?"

"Yeah, yeah, but there's a million women like her," Kruger said.

"If you do this for me," Samuels said, "the day you die, I'll be waiting for you. Do you know how much easier it's going to be for you with a friend like me there, an influential friend, a powerful friend?"

"Yeah, but still, what do I get out of it now?"

"Do this for me and I'll reward you beyond belief. I'll throw easy women at you all the time, the kind of women you like."

"Hmm," Kruger mumbled. "Reward beyond belief sounds pretty good. I guess the devil's right-hand man has some goodies in his pocket. I'll do it. You just better keep up your end of the bargain."

"Oh, I will," said Samuels, "I will." He briefed Kruger on everything he needed to know about Frances, and said at last, "One other thing. She still has a soft spot for her ex-husband. You're probably going to have to rip that out of her and make her resent him. I've seen you operate, and that should be a breeze for a seasoned veteran like you."

"No problem," said Kruger with a smirk.

Samuels left feeling confident that he was about to increase his winning streak to twenty-eight.

CR 9 RO

Kruger immediately went to work trying to win Frances over. He studied carefully all the information Samuels gave him about her. He signed up as a volunteer at several local children's organizations. He got a haircut and checked his wardrobe. The plot to destroy her soul had now become his own obsession.

He decided that it would be best to approach her in a public place so she wouldn't feel threatened. He followed her to the grocery store, filled his basket with items that a child might eat, and waited at the end of the aisle right next to hers.

When she came around the corner, he pushed his basket forward so that they collided, startling Frances. Kruger feigned surprised and said, "I'm so sorry. Are you all right?"

"I'm fine."

"I'm really sorry," Kruger said again. "I was a million miles away – I gotta finish getting all this stuff and get it over to the Shriner's Hospital by four o'clock. That's no excuse, though. No use doing something for one set of kids if you mow down another set in the supermarket. I hope your little boy and girl weren't too startled, and I hope I didn't break anything in your basket."

Frances, glancing up from making sure Ashley and Ryan were still beside her, noticed how handsome Kruger was. She hesitated a moment, then asked, "You work at the Shriner's?"

"Oh no, I just volunteer there," said Kruger smoothly. "But everybody there likes to chip in. This stuff I'm buying will be passed out at snack time so the kids can get a break from hospital food."

Frances looked in his basket and noticed that everything in it was child-friendly, like cereal and fruit snacks. She smiled and said, "Wow, you volunteer there? I wish more men were like you. I haven't known many that cared about helping children."

"Are you kidding?" Kruger said. "I'm involved with the Big Brothers program and Make-A-Wish. I used to work with the Boy Scouts, and now I'm in this program that provides social support for homeless children. It's the best thing – I wouldn't trade it for the world."

"Wow," Frances said. "It's an honor to meet someone like you. I'm Frances – Frances Fletcher."

"I'm James Kruger, pleased to meet you. What cute kids – are they yours?"

"Yes," Frances said. "This is Ryan. He's seven and this is Ashley, she's five."

Kruger extended his hand to Ryan; when Ryan went to shake it, Kruger pulled it away and said, "I got you." Then he pointed at Ryan, who laughed. Kruger extended his hand again and Ryan quickly grabbed it and shook it. Kruger said with a grin, "This time you got me."

Kruger turned to Ashley; smiled and said, "Hi, Ashley nice to meet you." He shook her hand without pulling it away, and then said. "I'll bet you have a lot of money." Reaching his hand behind her ear, he brought it back saying, "I knew you had a lot of money, look." In his open hand there was a quarter. He did the same to Ashley's other ear, then held out both quarters: "Here, you can have them."

Ashley checked her ears for more quarters and obviously found none. She looked to her mother for approval to accept the money; Frances nodded and Ashley shyly took the quarters. Ryan smiled and said, "Wow, Mister. Are you a magician?"

James laughed and said, "No I'm just an ordinary guy." James looked at Frances and said, "You're really lucky to have such great children. I bet you and your husband spend every waking moment with them."

Frances frowned. "I'm divorced. My ex-husband lives kind of far away and doesn't get to see them much."

"That's a shame," James said. "If they were my kids you couldn't keep me away from them. It must be hard being a single parent."

"It is, but I've learned to cope," Frances said." Well, we really have to get going now. It was nice meeting you."

"It was nice meeting you too," James said. "Hey, I was wondering if you'd want to go out for dinner sometime. I do Big Brothers on Tuesdays and Thursdays but I'm free on Wednesday. We can go someplace family-friendly, so you don't have to worry about finding a sitter."

Frances hesitated. *He seems nice enough and he likes kids. He's so good looking too. I haven't been out once since my divorce. Why not?* "Sure, we could meet you for dinner on Wednesday. What time and where?"

"How about five o'clock at the Pizza Palace. Then the kids can have fun and we can too."

"That would be great," Frances said. "We'll see you there."

Frances carried on with her shopping while James went to ring up all the items in his basket, which he was never going to use. He wanted to be sure to buy the items just in case Frances saw him leaving. On the way out of the store James rolled his eyes and thought, *Yuck. I hope I don't have to keep this up much longer.*

The next day Falco announced a revolutionary new computer chip, just as Josh had said they would. The stock went up twenty-eight percent near the end of the day. Timothy watched the stock all day and decided to sell right before the market closed. His company made another killing and it looked like Timothy could do no wrong.

Timothy knew that more investors would be calling after the news got out about how they did that day. The only problem was that they weren't the only ones who would notice. Timothy thought: *If I draw too much attention to our success then people are going to wonder how I can be so lucky. We might have to cool it for a while and only buy low risk stuff.*

He looked up and suddenly saw Alexander standing before him. Hiding his surprise, he said, "I was hoping you'd come back. I wanted to tell you to leave me alone and go bother someone else."

"You mustn't say that. I told you before that if you keep doing that I'm going to have to leave."

"I told you I want you to leave," Timothy said. "Take a look around. See this luxurious office and all the people I have working for me? We've just had the best few days ever and we're on a roll. I'm happy the way I am."

Alexander shook his head and said, "Haven't you learned anything since I've been here? Do you think you're going to keep on making money like this?"

"I've been making money my entire life like this, and finally when I make it big you come here to try to ruin it for me. I want to trade stocks and be left alone."

"So you think you did all this?" Alexander asked. "Don't you think it's a coincidence that all this happened right after I came?"

"Don't even tell me it was because of you," Timothy said. "You told me not to make the trades, remember."

"Exactly," Alexander said. "It was from the other side. Don't you see? You're being tempted with your first love – money."

"Now wait a minute," Timothy said. "I don't love money, and I deserve all that credit."

Alexander laughed and said, "You don't love money, right. Money is all you live for! Besides, the other side wants you to believe you did it all on your own. That way your ego helps you justify it." Before Timothy could get in an angry reply, he continued, "People make money all the time. Some people have made billions of dollars and they end up broke. You don't think that can happen to you?"

"They ended up broke because they weren't smart."

"Oh, and you are? Let me guess. You're too smart to go broke. Let me remind you that your company would've gone bankrupt a week ago if that illegal trade hadn't paid off."

"Hey, everyone makes trades like that," Timothy said. "Everyone who's anyone, that is."

"You have a warped sense of what's right and what isn't," Alexander said. "You need to learn a lesson or two."

"What could you possibly teach me about anything?" Timothy asked. "Do you know anything about the markets?"

"No," Alexander said. "I'm going to teach you something few men have ever learned. I'm going to teach you what's important in life. Men run around their whole lives chasing after money, and for what? To get more things that won't make them happy. Then they need more money to buy more things that they think are going to make them happy, which they won't. It's a never-ending cycle where men can never be happy because they always want more, more, more. The one thing in this world that is more precious than anything is time, and what have you done with it? You've wasted it. You can always make more money, but you can never get more time. It can't be bought, it can't be sold, and it's gone in the blink of an eye."

"So what you're saying is that mankind should give up everything they have so they can get more time."

"No," Alexander said. "Most people find a happy medium instead of working fourteen hours a day like you. What I'm saying is that time is the most precious thing there is. I've seen many men on their deathbeds and I've never heard one of them say 'I wish I'd spent more time at the office.' They always say 'I wish I'd spent more time with my family.'"

"Do you know what I've seen happen so many times? I've seen fathers neglect their children until they're teenagers, and then realize that their son or daughter is going to be gone soon. Then they try to jump into that child's life after the fact. What they don't understand is that teenager now has his own life that has nothing to do with his father. It doesn't work like that. You have to be part of a child's life from the beginning, or it's as if he doesn't know you."

Burning with guilt, Timothy said spitefully, "Maybe you should just leave me alone for good."

"If I leave before you change, you'll be doomed to hell."

"Well, maybe hell isn't such a bad place after all!"

"Do you know what it's like when you go down to the other side? You are tormented for eternity. The only exception to this is if they deem you worthy and send you out to try to steal a soul. Do you want to deal with that?"

Timothy, white as a ghost, murmured, "Just leave me alone."

"I'll leave you alone for a bit," Alexander said. "You don't have much time though. The other side sent someone to your wife and he's working on her right now. If you let him get control of her, it'll be over for her."

"Why should I care about Frances?" cried Timothy. "She took half of everything I had and moved away from here and took my children."

"For someone who runs his own business, you can be stupid at times," Alexander said. "You had a beautiful wife who gave up everything for you. She gave up her true love of teaching children just so you could be happy. She gave up her home and moved to a city she detested. She gave you two wonderful children who adore their father. And what did you do for her – buy her a new car and give her money? Please. Every time she begged you to move out of the city you ignored her. Weren't you listening? Didn't you hear the desperation in her voice? Or were you too selfish to give up one thing for her? I guess you were. And if you remember, you were the one that cheated on her."

Timothy's guilt was now overwhelming, and he shouted, "Get out of here, now!"

"Before I go, I want to say one last thing," Alexander said. "Time is going by fast, and before you know it, you'll be standing on Judgment Day with your eternity on the line. Your entire life will play in front of you, and you won't have any excuses. I hope you remember this day and this warning."

With that, Alexander disappeared, leaving Timothy alone and miserable in his office.

Kruger, knowing that the way to Frances' heart was through her children, went right to work. He met Frances, Ryan and Ashley at Pizza Palace for dinner with his pockets already filled with tokens for the game machines. He started playing games with Ryan and Ashley and barely spent time with Frances. After a little while they went back to the table and ordered their food and Kruger said, "You don't mind if I play a few more games with Ryan and Ashley do you?"

Frances looked at Kruger and said, "No go ahead." Kruger left and played several more games with them. He also played with them by chasing them through the tunnels and made sure they had a great time.

When the food arrived Frances was hardly able to persuade all three of them to sit down and eat. After dinner, Kruger gave Ryan and Ashley a handful of tokens each and Frances told them they could go play. After they left Frances said, "Thanks for asking us here. The kids are having a great time."

"No problem."

Frances shyly looked at him and said, "Can I ask you a personal question?"

"Sure, why not?"

"How is it that someone like you was never married? I mean, it just seems like you would've been married before."

"I guess I never found the right person," said Kruger. "Do you know how hard it is to find a person that has the same interests as you, someone who wants to raise a family and loves children like you do?"

"Actually I do," Frances mumbled.

"I'm sorry, what did you say?"

"Oh, nothing."

"You know, you really do have great kids. I'll bet they keep you busy."

"Oh they do," Frances responded.

Ryan came up to the table and said, "Mr. James, do you want to play the basketball game? I bet I can beat you."

Kruger looked at Frances and she nodded. Kruger stood up and said, "I'll bet you can't."

Ryan grinned, "Oh yes I can!"

Kruger thrilled Ryan by letting him win, then managed the rest of the evening in meticulous detail, even helping Ryan and Ashley turn in their tickets for prizes.

When it was time to leave, Frances said, "Thank you very much for showing us a great time. We really needed that."

"I'll tell you what," said Kruger. "You can pay me back by letting me take you out to dinner Friday night – just the two of us."

Frances hesitated. *He's so good with the children, and so good-looking,* she thought. The evening had made her realize how desperate she was for companionship. She said, "All right, I can get a sitter."

"Great," Kruger said. "I'll pick you up around seven. Oh, wait – I don't know where you live."

Frances wrote down her address and cell phone number, handed it to Kruger and said, "Seven o'clock will be perfect. I'll see you then." She left in a great mood and felt that maybe, just maybe, things were turning around for her.

Kruger picked up Frances on Friday night and again he turned on the charm. He took her to a nice restaurant called the Sky Gate. As they were being seated he asked, "Would you like a drink?"

Frances said, "I don't really drink, but I guess one glass of wine wouldn't hurt."

Yes, Kruger thought. *It's going to be so much easier if I get her to drink. Maybe I can eventually get her to start drinking every day. Then she'd be in the palm of my hand.*

"I'll have a glass too," Kruger said.

As they sipped their wine, he asked, "How are Ryan and Ashley doing?"

"They're fine," Frances said. "I have my friend Kelly watching them."

"Good. I'm so glad you could come out. Now, tell me about yourself."

"There's not much to tell," Frances said. "I was a school-teacher for seven years and quit when I got married. My ex-husband owns his own business and never had time for us. That's basically my story. What about you?"

"I guess I've lived a pretty normal life too," Kruger said. "I'm the top salesman at Barker Industries. They supply parts for everything from cars to washing machines. I like it a lot."

"Do you work a lot of hours?"

"Are you kidding? I'm not working my life away. I have too many kids at my charities that are counting on me."

Frances, starting to feel lightheaded from the wine, loved his answer. She smiled warmly at Kruger.

"I don't mean to be so forward," he said. "but you're very pretty. In fact you're one of the prettiest women I've ever seen."

Frances blushed and took another drink of wine and said, "You're just saying that."

"No, I mean it," Kruger said. "And you love children too. You're so good with Ryan and Ashley."

"Thanks," Frances said.

"I hope I can be half as good a parent as you if I ever get married," Kruger said.

Frances smiled and thought, *He seems perfect. He's polite, he loves children and he's so good looking.*

Kruger ordered two more glasses of wine when the dinner came. The evening passed happily and Kruger spared nothing to try to win her over. At the end of the night he walked her to her door, saying, "I had a great time."

Frances said, "So did I."

Kruger leaned toward Frances and kissed her on the cheek. She didn't resist and kissed him back. As she opened the door, he asked, "If you're not doing anything Sunday, do you, Ryan and Ashley want to go out?"

"This Sunday? Sure, what time?"

"I'll call you in the morning," Kruger said. "Count on having a fun day."

Frances smiled and went into the house, where Kelly was inside secretly watching. Kelly immediately said, "You were right. He is cute, and if he's as nice as you said, you might have a keeper."

"Stop," Frances said. "It's only our second date. But do you really think he's cute?"

"He's really cute," Kelly said. "Way cuter than that bum of an ex-husband of yours."

Alexander knew he had to act quickly. He appeared the next morning to Timothy, who was in his office preparing for a meeting. Timothy, busy and distracted, looked up, saw him and groaned, "Not right now, please."

"I'm warning you," Alexander said, "You have to get to your family and do something quickly. The person sent to Frances is fooling her and she's falling for him."

"Frances has a boyfriend?" Timothy asked. "Are you sure?"

"He's no boyfriend," Alexander said. "He's a despicable person who's going to try to bring Frances, Ryan and Ashley to the other side. You have to do something very soon."

"Now wait a minute," said Timothy. "How can one person bring anyone to the other side, especially a child?"

"Well, one person can't," said Alexander. "Mankind does have free will, and they can make their own choices. But one person can make someone so bitter and scar them inside so their past is difficult to overcome. Then they become vulnerable and easy to tempt with worldly things.

After that, it could take generations to remove the pain they have because it can be passed down from parents to children by the way they bring them up. The children become bitter and angry too. It's another one of those endless cycles I mentioned, just like your love for money."

"I tell you I don't love money," Timothy said.

"No, you don't love money. You just slave for it every day," Alexander said. "Oh wait. It's not money you love, it's the things that it buys and the power it brings. But we'll work on that later.

"One of your biggest problems is you're so bitter about your father supposedly treating your brother and sister so much better than you. Why do you still hold it inside you to this day? That bitterness inside has festered over the years so you turned to accumulating wealth to fill your void. But once you're bitter inside and refuse to forgive, nothing can fill that void, nothing but prayer. Besides, your anger is unwarranted. Your father was a great man and did you no wrong."

Timothy said under his breath, "Yeah my father, right."

"You really can't let go, can you?" Alexander asked. "All right then. I'm going to do something I'm not really supposed to do. I'm getting desperate and I have no choice. Close your eyes."

"Why?" asked Timothy, nervously.

"Just do it!"

Timothy closed his eyes and immediately flashed back to the day on the farm when he was a baby and he had the flu. It was in the middle of the night and he saw Gerald holding him and applying cold compresses to his head, just as Alexander told him before.

Now he saw Gerald holding him in a rocking chair, rocking and praying. "God, please don't take my son from me. I love him with all my heart. Please don't take him from me."

Now Timothy saw himself throwing away the pie he had stolen as a child. He saw himself telling a lie, and his father giving him more than one chance to tell the truth.

He saw Gerald talking to his mother after spanking Timothy for lying. Gerald had a tear in his eye and said, "That was the hardest thing I ever had to do. I love that boy so much, but I had to do it. I just had to."

Roberta said, "I know you love him, honey, I know you do."

"I hope he's learned his lesson about lying," Gerald said.

Now Timothy saw the day of the championship game, when neither of Timothy's parents was there to see him pitch. He saw his father holding Markus before he was supposed to leave to see Timothy play. Markus was barely breathing. Timothy saw his father's face ridden with anguish as he loaded him in the car and rushed him and Cindy off to the hospital. He saw Gerald pacing back and forth at the hospital, worried sick as he waited to hear from the doctor whether Markus was going to be all right.

Timothy saw himself and his father arguing after the championship game. Suddenly he couldn't take it anymore, and opened his eyes. His mind was blank and he couldn't speak.

Alexander looked up towards heaven and said, "Sorry, I had to show him. Don't be angry with me." Then he turned back to Timothy and said, "And this is the man you resented and didn't want to be like all these years. You ought to be ashamed of yourself. What kind of man did you choose to become instead? I'll tell you: the kind of man that turned his back on his father when he desperately needed you to keep the farm going. The kind of man who turned his back on his mother when your father died and she needed your help. The kind of man who turned his back on his sister and brother when they were in trouble. That's the kind of man you are."

Timothy sat wordless with a huge lump in his throat and a sick feeling in his stomach.

"Did I mention that the farm you grew up on is up for sale right now? But why should you care? You have all your precious money."

Timothy interrupted, "Hey, I gave my sister money when she needed it."

"That tiny amount you gave her? That was a drop in the bucket compared to what you were given."

Timothy looked startled. "I've never been given anything. I worked for everything I have."

"That's where you're wrong," Alexander said. "You were given the ability to make that money! That's right Timothy, *given*! It wasn't all on your own!"

"Your sister and brother struggle to this day and all you can think of is how you were treated as a child and how you can make more money instead of saving your ex-wife and children! I don't believe I was so naïve as to think you would ever change."

"What am I supposed to do?" Timothy asked. "Frances won't listen to me. She hates me."

"No!" Alexander said. "She should hate you for what you've done, but unlike you, she can forgive. She still loves you to this day, but you're too blind and obsessed to see it. If she falls in love with this other man, it's all over."

"How could I get her to listen to me?" Timothy asked.

"Oh, I don't know. Maybe you could tell her you're sorry for all the misery you caused her, and for being a horrible father." Alexander's face darkened. "You could even tell her you're less than a man because you won't fight to save your family. If it were a client you wanted to secure, you'd be on the phone doing everything you could to make sure you signed them, but the great rich Timothy Fletcher isn't man enough to fight for his family.

"You disgust me. Maybe I should give up and wash my hands of you. I would, if it weren't for the danger to Frances and your children. What's wrong, Timothy? Can't you say anything? Does the truth hurt too much? You may as well turn your back on them as you've done to everyone in your life except your clients."

And with that, he disappeared.

Timothy fell to his knees, trembling, and began to cry. He looked up and said, "I'm scared. I don't know what to do. Help me! Somebody please help me."

He heard Alexander's voice say, "If you had faith, you'd know what to do. When the time is right, you'll be tested. Your time is short so you'd better do something quickly. I can only help you so much. You have to prove you believe."

Timothy gained his composure and thought, *I'll go see Frances and see if what Alexander said is true. I'm not giving up all that I worked for my entire life though. I refuse to. My business is solid and I won't part with it and that's final. I'll go right after my meetings today.*

Timothy pushed ahead with his full day of client meetings. He could hardly keep his mind on his work; his normally fantastic presentations, which usually resulted in signing a client on the spot, faltered this time. One client after another blew him off with the fatal line, "I'll give you a call Monday."

When his meetings were over Timothy breathed a sigh of relief. For the first time in his life, he didn't feel bad about not closing a deal with a client. He was so enthralled with getting to the bottom of Alexander's words and proving him wrong that his business was secondary.

That evening Timothy drove to where Frances, Ryan, and Ashley lived. On the way he thought, *I'll get up there just in time to see Ryan and Frances before they go to bed. The timing will be perfect.* He took out his cell phone and called Frances. "Hey Franny, this is Tim."

Frances said, "You haven't called me Franny in years. What's up?"

"I'm driving up tonight. I was wondering if I could see Ryan and Ashley before they went to bed?"

"Sure," Frances said. "They'd really like that. Call me when you get in."

"I will," Timothy said, and hung up.

Two minutes later he heard a loud boom from the front of his car. It was a blowout in his front passenger side; he managed to swerve safely to the side of the road, got out and assessed the damage. He went to his trunk and pulled out his jack and spare tire.

When he went to change it, he saw that the spare was flat too. It had been in the trunk a long time, and he had never checked it. *A coincidence? I wonder. It seems that the timing of this is just too impeccable to be a coincidence.* He dialed up road service, who told them they would dispatch a tow truck immediately.

Timothy called Frances and said, "I'm going to be a little late. I had a flat tire and will be there as soon as I can."

"I already told the kids you were coming," Frances said.

"I'll be there soon," Timothy said.

"All right," Frances agreed and hung up.

About an hour later the truck still hadn't arrived. Timothy called again and demanded that a truck be sent out immediately. When the truck arrived the driver said, "Sorry it took so long. For some odd reason my dispatcher didn't get the message the first time." The tow truck driver tried to put air in Timothy's spare tire, but it wouldn't hold it. The driver had to tow Timothy's car to the shop, which was now closed.

Timothy was going to have to wait until the next day to get his car fixed which meant that he couldn't see Ryan and Ashley that night.

He called Frances and told her about his car.

She said, "The kids are going to be disappointed again. From now on, I'm not going to tell them you're coming until you actually get here."

"I'll be there tomorrow afternoon," Timothy said. "That's the best I can do, because the shop doesn't open until eleven on Sunday."

"Don't bother coming then," Frances said. We have plans tomorrow, and I'm not breaking them for a chance that you might come."

"I'll be there for sure tomorrow," Timothy said.

"No, I'm not breaking our plans."

"I have to talk to you and the kids about something," Timothy said. "It's important."

"If it's that important then you can talk to us tomorrow evening," Frances said. "I'm sure we'll be home by six."

"I'll be there tomorrow," Timothy said. "You can count on me this time."

As Timothy hung up, a strange feeling came over him. He felt as if his being held up was some sort of plot to deter him from seeing Frances. He couldn't explain why he felt that way; he just did.

He checked into a hotel and went into the bar for a drink. Alexander's warnings hadn't changed him completely; he gulped down six drinks before returning to his room.

The next morning Timothy got up late and went to the shop. By the time he got back on the road, Frances and the kids had already left home. Timothy tried to call her four times, but she never picked up her phone.

Kruger took Frances, Ryan and Ashley to a park a half-hour's drive from their house. They had a picnic lunch there, rented a canoe and paddled it down the river. Ryan was new to paddling and at first couldn't get the hang of it.

"Don't worry," said Kruger, showing him how to hold the paddle. "You'll be an expert in no time."

Frances felt happy that Kruger had taken an interest in Ryan. She thought, *This is exactly what he needs, a man to look up to, who can show him things. Timothy's never around and I feel bad for Ryan. I hope James asks me out on another date.*

After returning the canoe, the four of them played Frisbee and kicked Ryan's soccer ball around. After leaving the park, they went to a pet store and looked at puppies. Ashley saw a cute golden retriever. "Can we get him mommy, please?"

"No, we can't," Frances said. "Maybe when you get older."

"I love dogs," said Kruger. "I've always wanted a golden retriever."

"Don't encourage her," said Frances, rolling her eyes.

Kruger took Frances' hand and winked. "Yeah, maybe when you get a little older."

In the meantime, Timothy went over to Frances' house and waited outside since she wasn't answering her phone. At seven o'clock, Kruger finally pulled up in his car with Frances, Ryan and Ashley.

They all got out and went up to the house. The kids went in; Frances and Kruger stood on the porch and kissed; Timothy couldn't believe what he was seeing. Kruger grabbed Frances and pressed up against her body and gave her another long kiss.

Frances pushed him away and said, "I had a great time today, thanks."

"Anytime," Kruger said. "Can I see you tomorrow?"

Timothy jumped out of his car and ran toward the house thinking, *Is this the man that's going to corrupt my children? If so I'm going to put him down right here.* As he reached the porch he called, "Frances! Where have you been? I've been calling you all day."

"Oh hi, Timothy," Frances said. "I forgot to put my phone on charge and it was off all day."

Timothy said protectively, "Who's this?"

"Oh, I'm sorry I didn't introduce you," Frances said. "This is James Kruger. James, this is my ex-husband Timothy."

Kruger reached his hand out to shake Timothy's hand. "I'm pleased to meet you."

Timothy gave Kruger a dirty look and didn't extend his hand to shake. Frances said, "Timothy. Shake his hand."

Kruger quietly smiled ear to ear as if to say, *I have your ex-wife now and there's nothing you can do about it.* Timothy kept his hand back, and said, "Can I talk to you, Frances?"

"Sure. Hold on a second." She started walking Kruger to his car. Timothy was just barely able to hear what they were saying.

"He seems a little angry," said Kruger. "Are you sure everything is all right?"

"I've never seen him like this before," Frances said. "He's always so polite when he meets people."

"If you want me to stay I will," Kruger said. "I know how ex-husbands can be."

"No, that's ok," Frances said.

"Well, if you need anything you have my number. Hey, when can I see you again?"

"I'm free tomorrow during the day," Frances said. "The kids will be in school."

"I'll call you and we can go out to lunch."

"Fine, call me tomorrow," Frances said.

He got into his car and drove away.

Timothy nervously stepped up and said, "I don't like that guy at all. You have to stop seeing him right away."

Frances retorted angrily, "You have a lot of nerve coming here after we haven't seen you in four months, and telling me what to do! There's no way at all I'm going to stop seeing James. In fact, we're going out tomorrow."

"You don't understand," Timothy said. "He's no good. He's not what he seems."

"For your information, James is one of the nicest men I've ever met. He treats all three of us well. He's a real gentleman, unlike some people I know."

"Now wait a minute," Timothy said. "I always treated you well."

"Yeah, the whole three times you were home," Frances said.

"I deserved that," Timothy said. "I'm sorry for not being home enough, but you have to dump that guy. He's no good."

"Who do you think you are telling me who to date? We're not married anymore, remember. And where do you get off judging James like that when you don't even know him? I think you'd better leave right now."

Timothy grabbed Frances' arm. "You have to listen to me. You have to!"

Frances was shocked; Timothy had never touched her aggressively before. "You'd better let go of me now and get out of here," she warned, "or I'm going to call the police."

Ashley, hearing the commotion, came outside; her face lit up at the sight of Timothy. "Daddy, Daddy," she cried, running up to him.

Timothy let go of Frances' arm and swept Ashley up into his arms. "Oh honey, I missed you so much. I love you." He hugged her as hard as he could.

Frances was shocked at Timothy's display of affection. Why, after staying away so long, did he seem unable to let go of her? She squinted in disbelief and said, "Your father has to leave now. He came over to say hi."

"Daddy!" called Ryan, running up to join in on the hug.

Timothy swept him up along with his sister. "I missed you so much, big guy. I was wondering if I could come to one of your soccer games real soon?"

"Sure, Daddy," Ryan said happily.

"Don't do this to the kids," Frances said. "Don't get their hopes up and then not show up and crush them again."

"If I say I'm going to come to one of his games then I'm going to," Timothy said.

"You've promised things a thousand times before and never came through."

"I'm different now," Timothy said.

"Really?" said Frances scornfully. "Are stocks way up so now, you're different? And tomorrow stocks will be way down, and then you'll be the same again, is that how it works?"

Timothy was going to say something derogatory but held his tongue. He had to win Frances over, and knew he couldn't do it by arguing with her.

Frances was just about to ask Timothy to leave when Ryan saved him by saying, "I'm getting really good at soccer. Do you want to see me dribble the ball?"

Timothy said, "Sure, son." He followed Ryan and Ashley into the yard, where Ryan took the ball, maneuvered around Timothy and "scored." Timothy said, "Wow! You *are* good."

Ashley chimed in, "What about me daddy? Am I good?"

"Yes, you're good too," Timothy said.

"How come you don't come and see us much anymore?" Ryan asked. "Do you still like us?"

Timothy stopped and felt like his heart was going to burst. He called Ryan and Ashley over and said, "I love you two very much. I was really busy at work. I'll make sure I come to see you as much as I can from now on."

They continued to play soccer, laughing and joking for a half an hour, while Frances sat fuming. *I can't believe the gall of him, jumping in and out of Ryan's and Ashley's lives at his convenience and expecting everything to be great. I'm the one who does all the hard work of raising them.*

Frances finally said, "It's time to go in." Ryan and Ashley moaned, but she held her ground. "You have school tomorrow and I don't want to hear another word."

Timothy hugged both his children and said, "I promise I'll come back next weekend and visit. In fact, I'll be back every time I can."

Both Ryan's and Ashley's face lit up as Frances' darkened in disappointment. Frances escorted Ryan and Ashley into the house after that. After shooing them into the house, she turned to Timothy in disgust. "Why do you get their hopes up by telling them you're going to come back all the time when you know you won't? You don't know what it's like to see them get disappointed all the time."

"I'm not going to let them down again," Timothy said. "I've changed."

"Oh stop, Tim," Frances said. "It's late and I'm not in the mood for this."

"You have to stop seeing James," Timothy said. "I'm telling you he's no good."

"Stop it right now, Timothy, or I'm not going to let you come back over again for a while." She shut the door, leaving him standing on the porch.

Timothy drove back to the city that night feeling like a knife was being twisted in his stomach. The thought that Alexander could be right and the fact that his family could be in such peril nauseated him. Once home, he went right to bed and lay there thinking: *I just can't believe Alexander is an angel. He can't be. It's as if I'm in a bad dream or something. I wish I could wake up tomorrow and this would all be over.*

Meanwhile, Kruger was barely half way down the block when he pulled out his phone and dialed it. "Hey baby, this is James. What's up tonight?"

The woman said, "Hey James, how are you?"

"Good, good," James said. "I wanted to see if you'd like to get together tonight. We can pick up right where we left off, if you know what I mean."

"Oh I can't," she said. "My sister is in from out of town. Call me tomorrow though, and we'll get together."

"Okay, baby, I will," Kruger said. He dialed another number and another woman answered. Kruger said, "Hey, Angie. It's James. What's going on tonight?"

"Oh, nothing," said Angie.

"How about if I come over and pick you up? We can go out for some laughs, then go back to your place and hang out. What do you say, baby?"

"Sure," Angie said. "Can you come over in an hour?"

"I'll be there," Kruger said. "See you soon, girl."

10

The next morning Timothy drove to work thinking of what a great time he'd had with Ryan and Ashley; the best time he'd had in over two years, in fact. He felt guilty about all the time he'd missed with them thus far.

He could feel himself changing and was confused as to whether it was a good thing. He knew his business needed constant attention and he feared the worst; his college finance training had taught him to never stop striving to succeed. He saw his entire future in jeopardy if he didn't keep pounding away at the office; he wished he could come up with a happy medium between work and what was left of his family life.

Shortly after he got to the office, he had another phone call from his friend Josh. "Hey buddy. I have a real hot tip for you. It's only going to cost you twenty-five thousand this time."

Timothy thought for a moment: *I don't know if I should do it this time. I've done so well lately, why take the chance. But on the other hand, why not? Josh doesn't have tips every day* and he might not get one for months. I'm going to do it, absolutely.

"You know me," Timothy said. "I'm in."

"The company's name is Medrite," Josh said. "They trade under the symbol MRR. They manufacture medical equipment. They're going to make an announcement that they just signed a huge contract to do business with a Chinese firm. Their business is going to double. It's a medium-sized company now, but it won't be anymore."

"Thanks," Timothy said. "I owe you again, buddy."

"Just make sure you have the money in the account by the end of the day," said Josh.

"It'll be there," Timothy said, and hung up. After setting the deal up, he waited for the market to open. As he watched the countdown for the opening bell he thought, *Should I really be doing this? I don't know. Of course I should be doing this, everyone does. It's easy money and I have to. I'm going to do it and that's final.*

As soon as the opening bell rang, he executed the trade. He looked up from his computer and was startled to see Alexander standing before him.

"Have you learned nothing since I've come here?" Alexander reproached him. "Still making those trades, are you? When will you ever learn?"

"What's wrong with making a little money?" Timothy asked. "I had to do it. The information was there."

"Your life is about to fall apart," said Alexander, "and you think that accumulating more wealth is somehow going to fix things. Some people never learn – but *you* will, I promise you."

"What's that supposed to mean?" Timothy asked.

Alexander said, "I can't tell you anything else. It wouldn't matter anyway because you're so stubborn. I told you about the farm being up for sale and you did nothing. I told you about your sister and how she's struggling, and you did-n't help her one bit. I told you about Frances and you went there and made a half-hearted effort to talk to her."

"She wouldn't listen," Timothy said. "Why don't you just do something and make it better?"

"We can't interfere with the decisions people make," Alexander said. "Remember free will? We can only do little things to try to urge you to your destiny. Ultimately it's mankind that decides what to do. Besides, you're the one that needs to show faith.

"I can see this is going nowhere. You need a wake-up call and you're going to get one."

"What are you talking about?" Timothy asked. "I went to see Ryan and Ashley."

"I'm warning you that if she falls in love with James, it's all over," Alexander said. "You'll never be able to convince her then. You're going to have to do some soul searching today and figure things out for yourself." And Alexander disappeared.

Timothy shrugged off Alexander's words, unable to discern their meaning. He watched Medrite's stock all day; in the afternoon a press conference was announced, which was exactly what he was waiting for.

The CEO of Medrite went before the cameras and announced that an anticipated deal with a Chinese firm had fallen through. He also said that Medrite had had weaker sales than expected over the last quarter, and would have to downgrade its forecast for the next year.

Timothy gasped. He immediately put a sell order in, but by the time he could execute it, the stock price had fallen thirty percent. He lost nearly four hundred thousand dollars on the trade. He felt sick to his stomach and refused to take any calls.

He sat with his head in his hands for nearly fifteen minutes, trying to breathe normally again. Finally he thought, *All right. It was a bad trade. No big deal. We still have a huge amount of money from the trades I made last week. I'll make it up the rest of the week.*

Timothy's rational response to what happened was not nearly enough to make him feel at ease. He went to bed with a double dose of antacid tablets to try to get some relief. It didn't help much; he barely slept that night, worrying about his future. What he was too blind to see was that Alexander's warnings were slowly becoming a reality.

The next morning Timothy called Randy into his office and said, "I know yesterday was a horrible day for us. I guarantee today will be better. I want you to do me a big favor. I want you to buy a farm in Wisconsin for me. Here's all the information you'll need." He handed Randy a piece of paper.

Randy said, "Wow, sir, that's ingenious. Do you have a tip about the property having natural gas or oil on it? If so, you'll make a bundle."

"Never mind that," Timothy said. "I want you to call a real estate agent and set up a purchase agreement for full price with them."

"Full price, sir," Randy said. "It must be valuable if you're willing to pay that."

"You have no idea," Timothy said under his breath. "Let me know today what the price is and I'll prepare the check and pay for it in full. I'm going to take it out of my personal account. I want you to prepare the paperwork to have my ex-wife as the person that purchases it. She will be the sole owner with me having no interests at all in it financially."

"Do you think that's wise, sir?" Randy asked. When Timothy gave him a stern look, he quickly said, "Oh I get it, sir. You're going to do it for tax purposes. That way when you hit it big with natural gas you won't have to pay as much because your ex-wife's income level won't be as high. Wow, I guess that's why you're where you are today and I'm where I am."

Timothy nodded and said, "I want the sale rushed through and I don't want any mistakes. Make sure the title company starts working on it the moment the purchase agreement is signed. Do you understand? Now go and make this your top priority."

"Yes sir," said Randy.

With Randy gone, Timothy called Frances. "Hi Franny."

Frances said, "What do you want?"

"I wanted to let you know that I'm going to be there on the weekend to see the kids," Timothy said. "I was wondering if we could all go out together."

"You haven't come on your weekend in months," Frances said. "It is your weekend though, so I guess you can come. As far as doing something together, forget it. If you're going to have the kids then I'm going to make plans." A little spitefully, she added, "I do have a life of my own now, and I'm going to make the most of being free for the weekend."

Frances was definitely changing and Timothy felt it. Timothy knew his main purpose was to keep Frances and

Kruger apart so he quickly thought and said, "I was going to come and see them, but I can't take them for the entire weekend. I'm going to get a hotel room there and take them out and have a lot of fun."

"I guess if that's the best you can do, I shouldn't be surprised."

"Hey, Franny? There's something else. I need a really big favor from you."

"What is it now?" Frances complained.

"I allocated the funds for the purchase of the farm I grew up on as a child. I was wondering if you would close on it and put it all in your name."

"What is this, Tim? I thought you hated that farm."

"No. I don't hate that farm," Timothy said. "It's just… it went up for sale and I want the kids to have it. They deserve something for all the time I missed with them. Please do this one thing for me, Frances, please."

Frances sensed the desperation in his voice and knew it all too well. She remembered all the times she had sounded like that when begging Timothy to give up his business and to spend more time at home. She said, "All right. If it's for the kids, I'll do it."

"Thanks, Franny," Timothy said. "I owe you."

After Timothy got off the phone, he went to his bank and had a cashier's check for twenty-five thousand dollars made payable to his sister. He sent it to his sister's address with a note that said, "Cindy, I know you haven't heard from me in a long time. Please accept this gift from me. I hope it helps you out. Love, Tim."

Timothy spent the rest of the week trying to make up for the losses his company had incurred from the bad trade.

He didn't even come close to recouping all the money he'd lost, and wrote it off as a bad week.

When Timothy got the news about how much the farm would sell for, he prepared the check without questioning himself. He took the money and deposited it in an escrow account under Frances' name that was still open from when they were married. Then he waited for the announcement of a closing date.

Meanwhile, Kruger took a week off from work and spent it taking Frances out each day while the kids were in school. On Monday he took her to a romantic movie and held her hand during the sad parts. On Tuesday he took her to a Big Brothers meeting where kids were being assigned for the upcoming year. On Wednesday he took her to his sister's house to meet her small children. On Thursday he took her to a local school in an impoverished area and donated some new books. Frances was taken aback by Kruger's kindness at the school, and began to trust him more after that.

When Friday finally came, Timothy was excited. He couldn't wait to see Ryan and Ashley again; he hoped they could play soccer again and spend the entire weekend together. He arranged to pick up Ryan and Ashley shortly after six o'clock and after checking into a hotel went right over to Frances' house.

When Frances answered the door, he asked, "Can I talk to you?"

Frances said, "Sure. What do you want to talk about?" The door opened a little wider and he saw Kruger standing behind it.

With a lump in his throat, Timothy said, "Forget it. It can wait." Ryan and Ashley came running out; he hugged them and said, "I'm going to take you two out and we're going to have a great time," prompting squeals of delight from the children. They left with Timothy feeling very uncomfortable about Frances and Kruger being alone for the night. He had good reason.

Kruger and Frances stayed home and watched a movie. Kruger put his arm around Frances and kissed her; she didn't resist at first. He started getting more intimate with Frances and Samuels did his best to tempt her. *Just go for it. James is the one you've been waiting for. He's so good looking, and he's great with Ryan and Ashley. You'd better make your move now, or you might lose him. Let him have you now.*

No, Frances thought. *I can't do this. Not yet. I do like him, but what if Ryan and Ashley come home?*

Samuels continued pushing thoughts at her: *They won't be home for hours. Just go ahead. You haven't been with a man for so long.*

Frances thought, *No, not yet.* She pushed Kruger away, saying, "I can't yet. Just wait."

Normally Kruger would have kept trying with any woman that resisted. This time he held back, knowing Frances wasn't just any woman, and how important it was to get her to trust him. "I understand," he said. He couldn't believe he was hearing himself say what came next: "You take your time. When you're ready, you'll know."

Samuels smiled to himself. "We almost had her. It won't be long now."

Meanwhile, Timothy, Ashley and Ryan went bowling and had a great time. When they got back to the house, Timothy's fear that Frances and Kruger would still be together there was realized. As he took the children to the door, Ryan asked, "Daddy, can you come to my soccer game tomorrow? You did say you would come to one of my games."

"I'll be there for sure," Timothy said loudly, making sure Kruger heard him.

The next day Timothy went to Ryan's soccer game. Ashley sat with Timothy while Kruger and Frances sat apart, on the same side of the field. Timothy watched Kruger put his arm around Frances; his stomach churned at knowing that Frances was letting this outsider come into his family's life to destroy them. He thought, *I have to expose Kruger's intentions, but how?*

The game ended in a tie. Ryan came off the field and ran up to Frances and Kruger and said, "I tried really hard, but I didn't get a goal."

"That's all right," Frances said. "You had fun, didn't you?"

"Yeah," Ryan admitted.

It hurt Timothy badly seeing Ryan and Kruger together at a crucial time in Ryan's life. Timothy knew that after a sporting event was a good time to teach a child some of life's lessons. He felt left out and wished desperately it had been him talking to Ryan.

Ryan came over to Timothy and said, "Did you see me out there, Daddy, did you?"

Timothy felt a little better. "I saw you, son. You were great."

Frances and Kruger walked up and Kruger said, "The team is going out for ice cream. Do you want to go, Ryan?"

"Yes!" cried Ryan, running over to Kruger.

Frances looked at Timothy and said, "You can pick him up at our house in an hour."

Timothy nodded. Frances, Ryan, Ashley and Kruger all walked away. Timothy was bursting with jealousy, wishing it was him going for ice cream with his kids. When everyone got to their cars, Timothy couldn't take it anymore. He called out, "James. Can I speak with you a second?"

Kruger said loudly so everyone could hear, "Sure."

Timothy motioned to Kruger to step aside with him. The two walked about thirty feet away, near Timothy's car. Frances was putting Ryan and Ashley into the car and didn't pay much attention at first. Timothy said, "I want you to stop seeing Frances. I know who you are and who sent you, so leave my family alone."

Kruger remembered what Samuels said about having to make Frances hate Timothy, so he tried to provoke him by saying, "I'm not staying away from her. Who do you think you are?"

"I'm warning you to stay away from my family," Timothy said.

"It's not your family anymore," said Kruger. "Remember, you're divorced. I can't help it if you don't know how to treat a woman and satisfy her."

Timothy's face tightened and he was filled with a rage like he had never felt before. Unaware that Frances was now watching and unable to hold his anger in any longer, he shoved Kruger with his open hand. Kruger, seeing that Frances was watching, thought quickly and took a dive, banging into Timothy's car and falling to the ground. The fakery was only obvious to Timothy.

Frances ran up to Kruger and said, "Oh my gosh! Are you all right?"

Kruger made a loud moan in pain and said, "My arm, I think I broke my arm."

Frances bent down to help Kruger up and he put his other hand up to stop her. Frances tuned to Timothy and said, "How could you do that to him! What's gotten into you?"

Timothy tried to justify his actions. "He told me it wasn't my family now and that I should've taken care of you in the first place."

"I don't care what he said to you," Frances said. "That doesn't give you the right to hit him."

"I didn't hit him, I barely pushed him."

"I saw the way he went flying," Frances said. "You hit him badly, I saw. Come on Tim, at your son's soccer game? Get out of here, now!"

"But Frances, you have to listen to me," Timothy said.

"If you don't leave now I'm never going to speak to you again," Frances said. "Now go!"

Timothy realized he had no chance to change her mind, so he got in his car and left.

Frances turned her attention to Kruger and said, "Are you all right?"

Kruger said, "I think so," and struggled to stand up, wincing in pain. Frances helped Kruger up and asked, "Do you think you should go to the hospital?"

A light went off in Kruger's head and he said, "I'd better, just to be sure it's not broken." Frances helped Kruger get into the car and pulled out, heading for the hospital. On the way, Ryan asked, "What happened with Daddy? Is he all right?"

Kruger thought about bad-mouthing Timothy in front of his children, but then thought: *It's not time for that yet.*

Frances isn't quite hooked, but when she is, I'll have them hating their father. He grimaced a little in pain and said, "Oh, nothing happened. Your Dad just had to leave. He'll probably see you really soon."

Frances looked at Kruger in awe. *Timothy hit him and hurt him badly and he hides it to protect the kids' view of their father. Wow, I could've never been that forgiving. He's a much better person than me.*

Ryan asked, "Where are we going?"

"To the hospital," Kruger said. "I fell down in the parking lot and I think I broke my arm."

"Does it hurt?" asked Ashley.

"Yeah, kind of bad," said Kruger.

Frances, Ryan and Ashley spent three and a half hours in the hospital waiting for Kruger. When Kruger finally came out, his arm was in a sling. After he checked out Frances asked, "How bad is it?"

"I'll be all right," said Kruger. "I have to wear this sling for two days and then I can take it off. The doctor said that since it's not broken, I should use my arm as much as I can after tomorrow so it doesn't seize up. He said that it will be harder to get the full usage back if I wear the sling too long."

Frances took Kruger's hand and said, "I'm glad you're all right. I'm so sorry this happened."

"It's okay," said Kruger. "It's not your fault. I'm going to have to file charges against Tim just in case he tries it again."

"Do you have to file charges?" Frances asked.

"I'd better," Kruger said. "What if he beats me up worse next time? At least there'll be a record of it. I can always drop the charges after a while if he doesn't hit me again. His temper is obviously bad and there's no telling what he might do." He winced in pain again.

"I've never seen him act so violently," Frances said. "I don't get it." She sighed. "I'll drive you home. It's a good thing I drove to the game, or your car would still be at the soccer field."

"Thanks for being such a good friend," he replied.

When Kruger got home he took the sling off and tossed it on his bed with a laugh. He thought, *I'm a genius. I really am. I'll have Frances hooked before long and Timothy's kids will hate him too.*

That night Timothy went back to his hotel and was so upset he could hardly think straight. Every time in life before when he had a problem, he took control and solved it with money. This time he didn't know what to do. He was lost without a clue.

He knew Kruger would press charges; he could picture the ensuing trial as a fiasco. Kruger would make him out to be a bad guy and his children would think less and less of him. He pondered the situation for over an hour; the longer he thought about it, the worse things seemed.

He pulled out all the bottles of alcohol from the little wet bar that the hotel provided. He set them on the table and opened one of the bottles. He walked over to his suitcase and pulled out a bottle of pills again. He sat them on the table next to the bottle of booze.

Alexander appeared. "So you're going to give up without a fight. It doesn't surprise me."

"What am I supposed to do?" Timothy asked. "'Frances hates me and when Ryan and Ashley find out what happened they're going to hate me too."

"Frances doesn't hate you," Alexander said. "She still loves you."

"How do you know that?"

"That's not important," said Alexander. "The important thing is that she does. You asked what you're supposed to do. I'll tell you: you're supposed to be a man, like your father, and face your problems head on instead of with booze and drugs. If you have faith, you'll know what to do when the time comes. I've told you that." With that, he vanished.

Timothy sat alone most of the night worrying about what was inevitably to come. He knew he was going to have to face Kruger again and probably have to apologize to him in front of Frances. He finally listened to Alexander and tried to use what little faith he had. He prayed, "God, please help me. I don't know what to do. Please help me." He fell asleep riddled with anguish, not knowing that what had happened was nothing compared to what was to come.

❦ 11 ❧

The next morning Timothy woke up feeling unsure of his future, but tried to remain positive. He tried to call Frances, hoping that if he got her alone he could tell her exactly how he felt and maybe she'd listen. Her phone was off, so he drove over to her house. He knocked on the door and there was no answer.

It was Sunday morning and Frances, Ryan and Ashley were at church, but Timothy didn't know that. He waited outside, down the street a few houses in his car so he could catch Frances right when she came home. While Timothy was waiting Kruger pulled up in his car with his arm still in a sling.

Timothy watched Kruger knock on Frances' door and, on getting no answer, get back into his car and drive away. Timothy decided to follow him, being very careful not to be seen.

Kruger drove to a house just a few miles away; when he got out of the car he didn't have the sling on his arm. Timothy thought, *Oh you faker. I knew it.*

Kruger started walking up the sidewalk to the house and was met by a woman halfway up the walk. She hugged Kruger and they both went inside. Timothy thought, *I got you now you cheater.* Timothy wrote down the address of the house and took a picture with his phone just so he would have proof for Frances that Kruger was nothing more than a two-timer. Timothy drove back to Frances' and waited so he could catch her before she went in.

On the way out of church, Frances turned on her cell phone and called Kruger. "How are you feeling? Do you feel up to going out to breakfast with the kids and me?"

"I feel a lot better," Kruger said. "I'm still sore, but I was able to use my arm a little today. I actually took the sling off for a little while. I'd love to go out to breakfast with you three."

"Great," Frances said. "I'm sorry about the whole thing. Sometimes my ex-husband can be such a jerk. Meet me at my house so I can change and then we can leave from there."

"Sure," Kruger said, smiling. "I'll be right over."

When Frances came home, Timothy ran to the car before she and the children could even get out, as Kruger pulled up behind them. Giving Kruger a polite glance, Timothy said quickly, "Franny, I have to talk to you."

Kruger hopped out of the car with his sling on and walked up the sidewalk. Frances, startled, ushered Ryan and Ashley into the house, then turned back to Timothy and said, "What do you want?"

"In private," said Timothy.

Kruger went and stood by Frances. Frances said, "You can talk to me here."

Timothy looked at Frances and said, "All right then, I will. James is a cheat. I saw him go over to a woman's house this morning after he came here earlier. I followed him and when he got over to her house she came out and hugged him. He's two-timing you, Franny. I knew he was. I knew you wouldn't believe me, so I wrote the address down and took a picture so I could prove it to you." He handed her the piece of paper with the address and showed her the picture on his phone.

She looked at them, looked at Timothy in disgust and said, "That's James' sister. I was over there last week and met her. She's a really nice person and she has two children younger than ours."

Timothy stood there not knowing what to say. She continued, "Oh Tim, how could you? You were out waiting in front of my house and you followed James. You've become nothing more than a stalker. What's happened to you?"

"Wait," Timothy said. "I saw James take off his sling over there. He's faking. How do you explain that?"

"The doctor told him he had to start trying to use his arm without the sling," said Frances. "When I spoke to him earlier, he told me he took his sling off for a little while and that he was feeling much better. I can't believe you would follow him."

"I'm definitely thinking about getting that personal protection order I talked to you about yesterday," Kruger said. "You should think about it too, honey."

Timothy felt as if he would explode. *Who is he to call Frances "honey," and where does he get off talking to her about getting a personal protection order against me?*

He wasn't about to lay a finger on Kruger, knowing there would be a trumped-up charge if he did. Kruger took a step back anyway to emphasize the fact that Timothy had become unstable. He said, "Don't hit me again, please."

Frances stepped between them and said, "That's enough. I want you out of here before I have to call the police."

"Wait, Frances! You have to hear me out."

Frances sighed, then put her hands on her hips and nodded.

"You have to believe me that James is fooling you," Timothy said. "This is going to sound crazy, but a guardian angel came to me and warned me about James. He said that James was sent to you from the other side to steal your soul. He said a demon set the entire thing up to ruin our family. You have to believe me Franny, you have to."

Frances looked wide-eyed at Timothy. "Oh, come on Tim. You could've come up with something better than that. Do you really expect me to believe you? You're delirious."

"It's the truth," said Timothy.

"I'm sorry, Tim, but an angel was sent here for you? James is from the other side? That's ridiculous. James is one of the nicest people I've ever met. Have you been drinking again?"

As Timothy stood there speechless, Kruger couldn't pass up a chance to take one more jab at him and put the final touches on securing Frances. "I love you, Frances, but this is getting out of hand. I don't know if I can take Tim following me all the time and stalking me. I'm going through with the assault and battery complaint and the PPO."

Frances couldn't believe that James had said he loved her. She was so mesmerized by him now that she couldn't speak; her heart pounded and her face flushed. It had been so long since a man had said that to her; she missed the feeling of having a man around to take care of her and be a father to her children. She liked James now, and it didn't hurt any that he was such a gentleman and handsome.

"I tried to warn you," Timothy said. "You're going to have to live with what happens now."

"Is that a threat?" Kruger asked.

Timothy threw his hands up in the air and walked away.

Kruger said, "I'm sorry, Frances. I wish you didn't have to go through this. I feel like it's my fault."

"It's not your fault," said Frances. "I was the one that chose to marry him in the first place. Sometimes he can be such an idiot."

Now Kruger knew he almost had her. He thought, *It's only a matter of time before she falls helplessly in love with me and does exactly what I say. Things just got much easier.*

Timothy drove home feeling helpless. He had tried everything to make Frances see the truth, and still she couldn't see through Kruger.

Kruger spent the rest of the day with Frances, Ryan and Ashley, doing all he could to make it extra special. He thought, *If I can make them all forget about Tim for the day then I can make them forget about him for the week. He has to go to work tomorrow and he'll have to stay there and not come back until Saturday. By that time I'll have Frances under my control. She'll be telling me how much she loves me by then. She's almost there. I just need a little more time.*

He took them to a nearby carnival and spent plenty of cash to make sure everyone was happy. He won a stuffed animal for Ashley and let Ryan play all the games. They went out to a nice restaurant afterward and then back to Frances' house.

In Frances' backyard, as twilight fell, Ryan and Ashley kicked the soccer ball around while Frances and Kruger sat and talked. He said, "Thanks for such a great day. Your children are great; they're some of the best kids I've ever seen. If I had children, I'd want them to be just like them."

He knew this was the way to her heart, and sure enough, she was looking at him now as though her heart was melting. He moved closer to her and murmured, "I had a great week of vacation with you. I wish I didn't have to go back to work tomorrow. Ever since I met you, I've felt great about my life. My life has meaning now. You're the most beautiful woman in the world."

Frances' heart fluttered; she looked deep into his eyes and said, "Do you really mean it?"

"Of course I mean it. You're the most special person I've ever met. The way you treat Ryan and Ashley and never seem to lose your patience with them is incredible. You're awesome." He reached over and kissed Frances and she didn't resist. He pulled back, looked her straight in the eyes and said again, "I love you."

As Frances hesitated, Samuels went to work on her again. *Just ask him to spend the night. Put Ryan and Ashley to bed and you can be alone with him. It'll be the greatest night of your life. He said he loves you. You know you want him. Give in to him.*

Frances tried to fight off the thoughts: *No you can't. Just wait. If he loves you he'll wait.* Just then, Ashley came running up crying; Frances stood up and asked, "What happened?"

Ashley whimpered, "I fell down and hurt my knee."

Frances took Ashley inside and cleaned the cut and put a bandage on it, kissing it for luck and telling her it was "all better now." By this time it was dark out. She went into the backyard and said to Kruger, "I had a great time today."

Kruger smiled and said, "So did I. Will I see you tomorrow night?"

"What time do you think you'll get off work?"

"I should be out by five," Kruger said. "Can I come over after that?"

"Ryan has soccer practice at six," Frances said. "Then he'll probably have a little homework after that. If you want to come to his soccer practice you can."

Kruger thought about it: *I'm not going to be able to spend any time alone with her tomorrow. I may as well go out tomorrow night. My personal life is really suffering now and I need a night out.* He said, "Actually, I have a few things to catch up on after being on vacation; how about we make it Tuesday?"

"Definitely. I'll see you Tuesday. Call me."

When Frances went into Ashley's room to tuck her in for the night, Ashley asked, "Mommy, is Daddy all right?"

"Daddy is going through a rough time right now, probably at work," Frances said. "He's acting a little differently."

"How is he acting differently, Mama?"

"Oh, I don't know," Frances said. "He just doesn't think before he says things right now, I guess."

"Are you and Daddy going to get back together?" Ashley asked.

"I don't think so," Frances said.

"Why?" Ashley asked.

"Well," Frances said. "Mommy and Daddy don't like each other like that anymore."

"Daddy likes you a lot," said Ashley.

"What do you mean?"

"When Daddy looks at you, he looks at you funny," Ashley said.

"What do you mean he looks at me funny?" Frances asked.

"His eyes look different when he looks at you like he likes you a lot. I saw someone on TV who looked at someone like that before. Then they got married."

"What do you think of James?" Frances asked. "Does he look at me like that?"

"He kind of looks at you like that, but differently," Ashley said.

"What do you mean differently?"

"He looks at you like he likes you, but not the same as Daddy."

"You know an awful lot for a five-year-old girl, soon to be six," Frances said. "What do you think about James?"

"He's okay," Ashley said. "He's a nice man. He won me a stuffed animal today. He's still not like Daddy though."

"You go to sleep now and I'll see you in the morning," Frances said.

"Yes, Mommy," said Ashley and she yawned and closed her eyes.

The next day, when Timothy went into work, he called Randy into his office and asked, "Did you get everything done about that farm in Wisconsin?"

"Everything is done," Randy said. "All we're waiting on is the title work. I know you deposited the money in an escrow account in your ex-wife's name just as you said. I don't understand why. But I'm sure you have your reasons."

"Good work," Timothy said. "You can go now." Randy left and Timothy began his daily routine of checking stock prices.

Later in the day Karen told Timothy he had an important phone call. He picked up the phone and said, "Timothy Fletcher here."

Josh answered, "So professional, all for me!"

"I didn't know it was you," Timothy said, "What's up?"

"I have another deal for you," said Josh. "I got some information about a stock that should double in two days."

"The last stock you told me about was a bust," Timothy said. "My firm lost four hundred thousand on that deal. What happened?"

"It was the weirdest thing," Josh said. "The deal was all but done when someone from the Chinese firm got into an argument with someone from the American firm. They called it off after that. I've never seen anything like that happen in my entire life. Usually if companies are going to make that much money, they don't argue if everything's settled. It's as if the deal was destined not to happen."

Alexander, Timothy thought. *He said I needed to learn a lesson. I'll bet it was him.*

"We lost too much on that deal," Timothy said. "I haven't been able to make it up yet."

"I lost more than you," Josh said. "It's bound to happen sooner or later. Look how many deals were good ones. You know the risks in this business. Besides, you've made so many huge deals lately that you shouldn't be complaining."

"I'm not complaining," Timothy said. "I was furious when it happened though."

"This deal is a sure one," Josh said. "I need you to transfer twenty five thousand in the account by the end of the day."

Timothy hesitated and said, "I think I'm going to pass on this one."

"You're what?" Josh said. "I've never seen you pass up a deal like this before. Is everything all right?"

"Everything is fine. I just want to take a break for a while. I'm really busy with a family project right now."

"All right buddy," Josh said. "I'll catch you next time."

"See you later," Timothy said.

He hung up and felt great. He had done the right thing, the honest thing. He was pleased that he didn't have the burden of worry about if the trade was going to be a good one or not. He had forgotten how it felt to not have so much responsibility, to have a carefree lifestyle. Since he'd graduated from college, it had always seemed like he had the pressure of everyone's future on his shoulders. Every choice he made about what to buy and sell weighed heavily on him and he hadn't realized how burdensome it actually was until now.

He decided he wasn't going to make anymore insider trades unless he had to. He made a few minor trades that day and reviewed some of his clients' portfolios. At the end of the trading session, the company had lost a small amount of money. This would usually make him angry; not this time, though. For some reason he felt almost unaffected by the day's events.

He couldn't figure out why he felt so lackadaisical this time. He knew that almost all investment planners and stock brokers prided themselves in being right because that's how they maintained clients and got referrals. He realized it was because he had a bigger problem, and that was James Kruger.

Timothy thought about what his next move would be and came up with no answers. He remembered what Alexander had said to him: if he had faith, he'd know what to do.

As he was about to call it a day, his phone rang. "Tim Fletcher, how can I help you?"

"Hey buddy, how's it going," Josh said.

"Not bad," Timothy returned.

"You should've made that trade today," Josh said. "The stock went up forty-eight percent. We made a killing. You can't get cold feet when it comes to these deals. We're bound to get a bad one every once in a while. I'll call you next time."

"All right, see you later," Timothy said.

He second-guessed his decision as he always did. *I know I said I wasn't going to trade like that anymore, but I guess it wouldn't hurt. Maybe I will next time. I don't know.*

The next morning Timothy received a call before trading even started. The voice on the other end said, "Mr. Fletcher, this is Detective Michael Kensington with the Williamsburg Police Department. I'm calling in reference to a complaint that was filed against you for assault and battery. The plaintiff said the assault occurred at a soccer game on Saturday. I was wondering if you could come down to the station and answer a few questions."

"I can't come right now," Timothy said. "I'm at work and I live well over an hour away. By the time I get off today there's no way I could make it before dark."

"Can you make it tomorrow?" Detective Kensington asked.

"I have to work tomorrow too," Timothy answered.

"Well when can you make it here?" Kensington asked.

"I have the weekends off," Timothy responded. "I could probably come over Saturday."

"That's not going to be good enough," The detective said. "I'll have no choice but to put a warrant out for your arrest. We have a witness that saw the assault."

Frances was the only one that saw it, Timothy thought. *She didn't even see what really happened. Is she that far gone that she would corroborate his story?*

"What do you say Mr. Fletcher? Can you make arrangements to come sooner?"

"I'll have to look at my schedule." Timothy looked at his calendar and realized he didn't have that many appointments during the week. A strange feeling came over him that it was crucial to go there as soon as possible. He thought Frances was going to need him right away. He said, "I'll be there tomorrow around ten."

"That will be fine," said Detective Kensington. "I'll see you tomorrow at ten."

After hanging up, Timothy suddenly didn't feel so well. Assault and battery charges could mean negative publicity for his firm if it got out. Since he was dealing with someone that Alexander said was sent from the other side, he knew it was inevitable that it wouldn't be kept quiet. Timothy realized that corrupting his family wouldn't be enough for Kruger. He would try to ruin Timothy too, so he wouldn't have the power to fight back.

Timothy called Randy into his office and said, "I'm leaving you in charge for the next few days. I trust you completely. You're authorized to make trades as long as they aren't major ones. I'm going to ask you to meet with my clients this week as well. I only have three meetings over the next two days. I think you can handle it. Just tell the prospective clients that I was called out of town on a family emergency. If they're decent people they'll understand."

"You've never given me that type of authority before," Randy said. "I won't let you down."

"Good," Timothy said.

"Is everything all right, sir?" Randy asked. "I've never heard you talk like this."

"How so?" Timothy asked

"I've never heard you say things like if they're decent people they'll understand or that you trust me completely. You've always said you never trust anyone completely in business."

"Maybe it's time for you to play a bigger role around here," said Timothy. "I have to go now and make some personal arrangements. Don't worry. Everything is fine."

Timothy spent the night trying to figure out a way to expose Kruger for what he truly was. Little did Timothy know that the plan he would eventually come up with would blow up right in his face.

✺ 12 ✺

The next morning, Samuels appeared to Kruger and said, "You almost have Frances. She grows weaker every time she sees you. You must get her to submit willingly, and soon."

"I'm trying."

"You need to try harder," said Samuels. "You need to do something with her children that will make her sure that you're the one she's been looking for."

"I don't know how long I can keep this up," said Kruger. "I've done everything I can with those little monsters."

"Listen," Samuels said. "The key to getting someone to do exactly what you want them to do is to exploit their weaknesses. Everyone has vices and you have to inflame their desires for those vices. Some people love money and others can't resist alcohol; you can't say no to women. If you learn how to exploit people you can get anything you want. I can only put tempting thoughts in her head to help. So now you have to figure out a way to get Frances to surrender herself to you. You'll think of something."

Meanwhile, Timothy set out for the Williamsburg Police Station. On the way, he thought about how to prove to Frances that Kruger was a fraud. He decided that he had no choice but to follow Kruger again and try to catch him in the act of doing something devious. Then he could present concrete evidence to Frances and she'd have to believe him.

He walked into the police station and asked to see Detective Kensington. The detective came out and introduced himself, leading Timothy to his office in the back of the station. He offered Timothy a cup of coffee, which Timothy politely declined.

"I'm going to get right to the point," Kensington said. "I have a complaint that was filled by James Kruger stating that you assaulted him last Saturday afternoon. Is this true?"

"No," Timothy said.

"I believe there was a witness," Kensington said. "It was your ex-wife, Frances Fletcher. She said she saw it, but she wouldn't write a statement against you. Why don't you tell me what happened in your own words."

"I went to my son's soccer game and afterward I asked to talk to James. When we went over to talk he started to insult me and that was it."

"Did you push him?"

Timothy thought, *If I tell the truth, I'm going to get in a lot of trouble and it could possibly affect my business. If I lie, Frances will never believe a word I say again. It's more important that I get through to Frances right now. I just have to.*

"Yes, I pushed him," Timothy said. "It wasn't like you think, though. He said that my children weren't mine anymore and that my ex-wife was his. I pushed him, very lightly, and he acted like he was hurt. The dive he took was completely fake. You don't know how he is. He's a really bad person."

"I did a little checking on Mr. Kruger and he seems pretty normal to me. He doesn't have an adult criminal record; he has a full-time job and does pretty well."

"I know he looks great on paper, but you don't understand."

"Why don't you explain it to me, Mr. Fletcher?"

Timothy started to say, "You see," and then thought, *I can't tell him about Alexander. He would think I'm nuts. I have to say something though.* "I can't explain it right now. You just have to believe me that he's no good."

"I see," Kensington said. "Well, anytime you lay a finger on someone it can be construed as an assault. The fact that you pushed him means you committed a crime. I pulled your criminal record as well. It seems that you're clean too, except for the one DUI."

He glanced again at the report and continued, "I wish you two could settle this as gentlemen, but Mr. Kruger insisted on pressing charges. He seems to feel that you're a very dangerous person. He claims he has to file this complaint because he thinks you'll probably assault him again. He also claims you were stalking him after the incident. Is this true?"

"No it's not true," Timothy said. "I can't help it if he was over at my ex-wife's at the same time I was."

"He said you followed him to his sister's and was watching his every move. Is that true?"

"Well, no…"

"Just how was it then, Mr. Fletcher?"

"I'm not saying anything else until I talk to my lawyer," Timothy said.

"You can talk to your lawyer," Kensington said. "It looks like we're going to have to go through with this case. I'm going to charge you with assault and battery."

"I didn't assault him, but I guess you're going to believe him."

"You say that you pushed him and your ex-wife saw the whole thing. You didn't deny that you were following him. And your wife says you've been acting very strange lately. Who would you believe?"

"I'd believe me," Timothy said.

"Well, I'm going to charge you now and talk to the prosecuting attorney about letting you go on a five hundred dollar personal bond," Kensington said. "I can't get you in front of the judge today, but you should be arraigned tomorrow. From what your ex-wife tells me, you're a very successful financial planner and stockbroker. I don't think you'd be stupid enough to not show up for court tomorrow morning, unless you want to sign a confession right now. I could probably get you probation." Timothy shook his head.

Kensington said, "I didn't think so. I don't think you're a threat to society, so I'll go ahead with this plan. By the way, Mr. Kruger is requesting a PPO against you for his own safety. It'll be up to the judge tomorrow.

"A word of advice to you, Mr. Fletcher." Timothy raised his eyebrows. "Don't get involved in a domestic dispute with your wife or her boyfriend again. I've seen hundreds of these cases, and the ones who always end up getting hurt are the kids. Don't do anything stupid for their sake." Timothy didn't say a word.

Kensington said, "Can I speak off the record, Mr. Fletcher?"

"Go ahead."

"I know you're probably jealous of your ex-wife's boyfriend, but things in life happen. Just let it go. If you really want her back, you can do it by being a good guy, especially to your children. One other thing: I don't trust Kruger either. There's something about him I don't like. I've been a detective for fifteen years and I can read people. He seems like he's hiding something. That's between you and me. I have to follow the law though, so let me go see what I can do."

The prosecuting attorney asked Timothy to sign a few papers and sent him to the cashier to post a small bond. He was to report to the court in the morning at eight-thirty for arraignment.

He left the police station, checked into a hotel and called Randy to tell him he wouldn't be back for a few days, and to do the best he could without him. Randy told him that everything was fine, which eased his mind; at least one thing in his life wasn't falling apart.

Timothy called his long-time close friend John Jacobs, who had handled his divorce. John owed Timothy a few favors because he had made him so much money in the past, setting up a lucrative college fund that would provide all three of John's children with full tuition. Timothy explained the situation and John agreed to drop everything and meet him in the morning at the courthouse.

Timothy knew he still had to get something on Kruger and fast. He realized Frances was falling for him, because he was able to talk her into going to the police station and corroborating his story. He remembered what Alexander had said: if she fell in love with him, there was no turning back.

He felt more desperate than ever, knowing his children's future was at stake.

Frances had previously told Timothy where Kruger worked, so all he had to do was find out where the building was. Just before Kruger got off work, Timothy went down to his office building and waited outside for him. When Kruger eventually came out, Timothy carefully followed him to what apparently was his apartment. He waited patiently outside for a little while desperately watching and hoping for some kind of break.

Kruger must have spotted Timothy on the way home, because about twenty minutes later a police car pulled up next to Timothy's car. Two police officers got out and one of them asked, "May I see your license and registration, please?"

Timothy asked, "Can you tell me what I did wrong, sir?"

The officer again said, "Can I see your license and registration, please. And please step out of the car."

Timothy got out of his car, pulled out his license and registration, and handed them to the officer, who took them and said, "Wait here. I'm going to check this out. I'll be right back." The other officer stayed with Timothy and asked, "What are you doing here?"

Timothy said, "I'm just parked, that's all."

"Do you know anyone around here?" The officer asked. "No."

"Then what are you doing here?"

Timothy went on the defensive, "Can you tell me what I did wrong?"

"We had a call that you've been following someone who lives in that apartment complex across the street. That's the second call we had from that person in under a week. It seems funny that you're here when we had a call about it."

Before Timothy could answer, the other officer came back and said, "No outstanding warrants. He's clean."

The officer questioning Timothy was just about to continue when Kruger ran up, yelling, "This is the guy I called about! He assaulted me the other day and followed me twice now. He's stalking me. I petitioned the court to get a personal protection order, but it hasn't been signed yet. You can check it out with Detective Kensington."

Timothy scowled at Kruger, who backed up a little. The officer questioning Timothy said to Kruger, "This is a public street and he has a right to be here. Until you get that PPO I can't do anything. We can document this though, and when the order goes before the judge this incident will help him decide on signing it."

Kruger wickedly smiled as if to say to Timothy, *I've got you now.*

The first officer said, "Mr. Fletcher, I suggest that you move along. If I have to, I can take you down to the station for questioning. Since there was a charge of assault and battery filed against you the other day, this could be construed as harassment. What's it going to be? Are you going to leave, or do you want to go downtown? It's your choice."

Before Timothy could give the officer his decision Kruger interrupted, "I think you need to take him downtown for my safety."

"I'm leaving now," said Timothy.

The officer handed back his license and registration, saying, "If we find you over here again we're taking you in. Do you understand?"

"Yes."

"Okay. Now go."

They pulled away from his car, and he got in and drove away, leaving the two officers talking to Kruger. Timothy drove back to the hotel and called Frances, hoping to catch her before Kruger called her. When she answered she said, "I can't believe you did that to James again. What's wrong with you?"

"Let me explain," Timothy begged. "James is a really bad person and I'm trying to stop you from making the worst mistake of your life. He's from the other side..."

Frances cut him off right there. "Not that crazy story again about angels and devils. James is one of the most decent men I've ever met. He works with children and he treats Ryan, Ashley and me like we're special. I've known you for a long time, Tim, and I hate to say this, but you need professional help. I have no choice but to go to court and try to have your visitations supervised."

Timothy felt like his heart would explode. Although he had put so much effort into his business year after year, he now knew that his children meant the world to him. "No Franny, not that," Timothy said. "I still love you." Frances paused for a moment, surprised at Timothy's candor. Timothy hadn't said that in years and it shocked her.

"It's over between us, Tim. I tried to make it work. I have a good life now. You have your own life too. Please leave James alone, please. I have to go now. Take care." She hung up.

Timothy's stomach was churning; he felt like throwing up. He couldn't believe that he was possibly going to lose his right to see his children unless someone was watching his every move.

He tried to go to sleep that night but lay awake with worry. He finally got down on his knees and prayed, "God, help me. Please don't let Kruger win Frances over. I need your help. I'll do anything if you help me, please."

When morning finally came, he was tired and grouchy. He got up and met his lawyer down at the courthouse. When John saw Timothy he said, "I read the police reports about what happened. What's going on? Did you do all those things in the reports?"

"I guess so," Timothy said. "All except the assault."

"Tell me exactly what happened and don't leave anything out."

Timothy explained exactly what happened, being very accurate, except for one detail: he didn't mention Alexander, for fear John would think he was crazy. If Frances didn't believe him, there was no way John would.

After he was done telling the whole story, he thought for a moment. *Maybe Frances is right. Maybe I do need professional help and I am going crazy. After all, Alexander hasn't appeared to me in quite a while and who's to say if he's real or if he's just a hallucination. He was right about so many things though. I just don't know about anything anymore.*

John abruptly asked, "What's happened to you? Are you all right? You're one of the most responsible, level-headed people I know, and you're running around like a teenager in love for the first time. You were stalking your ex-wife's boyfriend, really? I thought you couldn't stand her anyway. She did take half of everything you had, you know. I suggest you go back home and date one of the many very nice women you know, and forget about your ex-wife."

"I can't forget about her," Timothy said. "You don't understand."

"I do understand one thing," John said. "If you keep this up you're going to lose everything you've worked for. Do you want this to get out? Do you think anyone is going to want to open an account with you if they think you might stalk them? Come on, Tim. Get it together." Timothy sat silently gazing past him.

"Just let me do the talking when we go before the judge," John said. "I know the charge is a misdemeanor, but we're going to plead not guilty on this anyway. I don't see any other choice. If this gets out it could kill your career. You know what bad publicity will do to a business like yours. People wouldn't care about it if you were in just about any other field, but when you handle their money, they take heed. Don't worry, I'll put Kruger on the stand and tear him to shreds. When I'm done with him, he'll be asking for his mommy, he'll be so confused."

When it was time to go before the judge, he said, "Timothy Fletcher, you are charged with assault and battery. How do you plead?"

John said, "My client pleads not guilty, your honor."

"Is this correct, Mr. Fletcher?" Judge McKinney asked.

Timothy cleared his throat and said, "Yes, your honor."

"We'll set trial for the sixteenth of next month," Judge McKinney said. "Is that fine with both attorneys?"

John said, "It's fine with me."

The prosecuting attorney gathered a few papers and said, "The date is fine, your honor, but there is another issue here to be taken into consideration. The plaintiff has filed for a PPO against Mr. Fletcher. Mr. Fletcher was apparently in front of Mr. Kruger's apartment yesterday and was seen following him two days prior. Two officers were called to

Mr. Kruger's address and verified that Mr. Fletcher was there."

"Mr. Fletcher, were you in front of Mr. Kruger's home yesterday?" Judge McKinney asked.

"Yes, sir," Timothy said.

"And what were you doing there?"

"I was just parked," Timothy said.

"Were you following Mr. Kruger," Judge McKinney asked.

Timothy wanted to lie but he knew he was under oath and said, "Yes, I was sir."

"And why were you following him?"

John interrupted. "My client wants to exercise his right to remain silent."

"Very well," Judge McKinney said. "Considering the circumstances, I'm going to sign the PPO against you, Mr. Fletcher. You are not to come within five hundred feet of Mr. Kruger at any time. If you violate this order, I will have you back in front of me and I won't be as lenient as I'm being now. Do you understand what this order means, Mr. Fletcher?"

"Yes, your honor," Timothy said.

"Then I will see you on the sixteenth of next month, Mr. Fletcher."

Once outside the courtroom, John said, "Don't go within five hundred feet of that guy again, and get back to your business where you belong. If you do violate the PPO you'll end back up in court and you might do some time." He smiled. "Besides, my money is sitting in an account at your firm and it needs you to make it grow. You're the best financial planner I've ever met, Tim. Don't jeopardize your future for some loser who doesn't even matter."

As they left the courthouse together, John continued, "I've known you for a long time. I know you're not crazy. If you really want to get this guy, hire a private investigator. I know a guy that could find out what Kruger ate for lunch on the first day of school in the third grade. He's that good. I've used him many times on cases before." He wrote down a name and a number. "Here, you're one of the smartest people I know. Use your head and let someone else do the dirty work. Now get back to your business and forget about this nonsense, and most of all stay away from Kruger."

Timothy got in his car and thought, *John's right. Why didn't I think of that before? I guess I was so obsessed with proving Kruger was a fraud that I didn't think of hiring a private investigator. I'm going to call this guy as soon as I get back to the hotel.*

Meanwhile, Kruger went over to Frances' house. On the way he thought about what Samuels said about getting Frances to trust him. Kruger had a plan that he believed would hit Frances right in the heart and make her give in. When he got to her house he picked up a book and asked Ashley if she wanted him to read her a story. Ashley, of course, said, "Yes."

Kruger read Ashley the story, joking and laughing the entire time. Then he pulled out another book and said, "I'm going to teach you to read." Since Frances was a former teacher she was touched by this. "This book is called *The Cat in the Hat* and you can have it when I'm done. It's a book specially made for really smart people like you to learn how to read. I'm going to sit here as long as I have to until you can read most of the book."

He sat with Ashley for two hours until she could read a good portion of the first part of the book. Frances smiled as she watched them, wrapped in a warm glow. As they were winding down, Frances thought: *James is the best thing that's ever happened to me. I couldn't ask for a better man. I'm lucky to have found him. I can't resist him anymore. I know he's the right one.*

Kruger told Ashley, "I'll sit down and read with you every day until you're the best reader in the state. In no time you'll be able to read huge books." He sent Ashley off to play, turned to Frances and said, "She's wonderful. So smart, too. Your kids are the best."

Frances could barely resist Kruger anymore. If Ryan and Ashley hadn't been there, she might have given in to him on the spot.

Timothy called the number John gave him and asked to speak to David Randolph. After a moment, a man answered and said, "Randolph here, how can I help you?"

Timothy explained the entire situation.

Randolph said, "I charge five hundred a day plus expenses. I'm the best there is and if this James Kruger is as you say he is, then I'll get him the moment he does something wrong. You'll have pictures, dates, times, places and names of who he was with. I'll know how many times this guy burps a day after a week."

Timothy was impressed at Randolph's confidence, and since the man came highly recommended, he said, "You're hired." He gave Randolph all the information about Kruger.

Randolph said, "I can't start for three more days, until I wrap up the case I'm on right now. It won't really matter, because if he's going to do something it's probably going to be on the weekend; you said he works all week during the day anyway. It wouldn't make a lot of sense to wait outside his office building during work hours. I'll get on it Saturday."

"I want to let you know, Mr. Randolph, that I take care of people that take care of me," Timothy said.

"You'll be hearing from me, Mr. Fletcher," Randolph said.

Finally, a break, Timothy thought. *I'll get Kruger if it's the last thing I do.* He was putting all his hopes in Randolph; he should have put his faith first like Alexander told him. He was now counting on a man to save him and his family instead of counting on above.

Timothy was now confident that things were going to turn in his favor, so he did what John suggested and drove home. He had a renewed hope in Randolph that made him able to function rationally again.

In fact, he was so confident that he decided to call Frances that night. He figured he would try to get her to listen to him one more time. "Hi Franny," he said when she picked up.

"What do you want?" Frances asked.

"I was hoping you'd talk to me for a minute and let me try to explain one more time."

"I don't want to talk to you right now," Frances said. "I heard you pled not guilty to the assault and battery charge today. How could you lie like that? I saw you assault James."

"You only saw the tail end of what really happened," Timothy said. "Kruger is lying to you. You have to hear me out."

"Not that again," Tim. "I've heard your ridiculous story one too many times."

"Please Franny, just listen," Timothy begged.

"I won't do it, Tim," Frances said.

"I'll be over to see Ryan and Ashley this weekend," Timothy said. "It's my weekend to see them."

"About that," Frances said. "I think it's a good idea if you don't come over to see the kids for a while. Considering all that has happened with the assault, I think its best that way."

"Don't do that, Franny," Timothy pleaded. "Ryan and Ashley are all I have right now."

"You mean to tell me you didn't care about seeing your children for months, and then all of a sudden when I get a boyfriend it's the most important thing in your life? What about your precious business that I asked you to give up so many times? Don't you still have that? Aren't you still in love with your firm?"

Timothy's body felt empty inside. That comment hit him hard because he knew it was true. Timothy finally realized how much he had neglected his wife and children, and knew just how wrong he was. He also knew that Frances was changing for the worse. From what Alexander had told him, Kruger would have his claws in Frances and have her turned the other way in no time.

"No, Tim. I won't let you see Ryan and Ashley this weekend," Frances said. "You may as well know that I'm going to ask for supervised visits for a while. I'm going to try to get your visitation rights cut to once a month. James and I decided that would be best."

Timothy was furious. "So James helps make decisions about my children now? It's my weekend and I want to see them."

"If you must know," Frances said. "James, Ryan, Ashley and I are going to spend the weekend together. He's taking us out all day Saturday and all day Sunday. He's so creative. So don't bother stalking us. I'll call the police and have you arrested if I have to."

"Please, Frances, can't you see what's happening?"

"I see what's happening," Frances said. "I'm trying to make a good life for our children and you're trying to stand in the way. I have to go now. If you bother us this weekend I'm going to ask for a PPO too. I don't want to, but I'll have no choice." She hung up, leaving Timothy holding the phone feeling distraught and hurt.

Oh no. What good will it do to hire Randolph if Kruger is with Frances all weekend? He won't do anything wrong. If Randolph watches him during the week he won't find out anything either because he'll be at work. By that time it'll be too late. Randolph was my only hope.

Frances has changed so much from the person she used to be. I realize now Alexander was right that it's going to affect the way that Ryan and Ashley grow up. What am I going to do?

If I wait and do nothing, Frances will have totally fallen for Kruger by then. If I follow them it's going to be worse than before if I get caught. I don't know what to do.

Temptation set in just then, as it always does when someone is at their weakest and most vulnerable. A thought popped into Timothy's head: *Just give up. You've lost. Focus on your business. If you do it'll grow beyond your wildest dreams. You'll have more money than you ever thought possible. You know with money comes power. You'll be praised as one of the greatest investors of our time. You'll have the finest things money can buy. You'll have the most beautiful women in the world, plenty of them. Just forget about Frances. She's changed and she's never going to change back. Give up and you'll have everything you've ever dreamed of.*

"No!" Timothy screamed. "I'll never give up. I've never given up in my entire life and I won't start now. Be gone from me, you devil! I know about you. I will fight to the end."

Another thought entered Timothy's head: *Have it your way. You'll be sorry when you're begging for help. Frances is lost and so are your children. I'll make it so Frances will never let you see them again unless you give in to me right now.*

"Be gone," Timothy yelled. "I know I have free will and you can't make me do anything I don't want to. I won't give up. I won't!"

Timothy had been tempted with all the evil and riches the world had to offer and still he had resisted. The test he had just passed was one failed by so many men. His faith had saved him. He fell to his knees crying and prayed, "Help me, God. Please help me. I don't know what to do next."

He prayed longer than he ever had in his life. He was so upset that he felt little comfort in his newfound fragile faith. Nothing he had ever done in his life had prepared him for this agony. Little did he know that the worst was yet to come. He would have to pull every bit of faith, strength and self-control he had from his inner soul to survive the evil that Samuels had planned.

His only comfort came right before he went to sleep. He remembered Alexander's voice saying: *If you use faith, you'll know what to do when the time comes.* Timothy thought, *I'd better know what to do, because all our lives depend on it.*

❧ 13 ❧

The next morning, Timothy went to work and shut himself up in his office. When Randy came to fill him in on the events of the week, he barely listened. Randy asked, "Is there anything wrong, sir?"

"No, you did a fine job," said Timothy. "Now go, and leave me alone; I have a lot to think about." Randy left, worrying about his boss and long-time friend. Timothy spent the rest of the day in a daze, not getting anything accomplished.

Ryan and Ashley came home from school. After grabbing a snack, they asked to go outside and play as usual. "Remember the rules," said Frances. "You can go as far as Mrs. Johnson's on the left side of the block and as far as Mrs. Cranston's on the right."

"We know, Mommy," they said in unison, and went outside, where Ryan began practicing his soccer moves on the front lawn.

Ashley got on her bike and began riding up the sidewalk. Still new to riding without training wheels, she pedaled up to the corner and, instead of executing a tight turn, veered down the curb and cut into the street, which was strictly forbidden. Without looking ahead, she cut between two parked cars and pulled out into the open street, right in front of an oncoming car.

The man in the car slammed on his breaks. It was too late. He ran into Ashley, throwing her six feet sideways. Ryan spun around just in time to see her hit the concrete. He screamed and ran to Ashley; Frances heard the scream from inside the house and came running out.

Frances saw Ashley lying on the ground, still and lifeless, and screamed. The driver ran up and said frantically, "I didn't see her. She rode between two cars and I couldn't do anything. I wasn't speeding or anything. Why did this happen, why?"

The man dialed for help on his phone while Frances knelt over Ashley, weeping as she tried to find a pulse. "Oh no, God," she whimpered, "don't take my baby. If you have to take someone, please take me. Please God, take me instead, please." She wailed as Ashley lay in the street limp and unconscious.

The driver, also in tears, knelt beside her as they waited for the ambulance. Ryan couldn't face seeing his sister lying there; he ran into the house crying, went up to his room and prayed for help for his sister.

At the hospital, Frances called Timothy from the emergency waiting room. "Tim! There's been an accident. Ashley was hit by a car. We're here in the emergency room – she's fighting for her life."

In tears, Timothy cried, "How did this happen? Was the driver at fault?"

"No, he couldn't see her. He wasn't doing anything wrong."

"Well what was she doing riding in the street?"

Frances wailed, "I don't know what she was doing riding in the street. I've told her a hundred times not to do it."

Timothy recognized the desperation in Frances' voice. He remembered it from so many times in the past when Frances had pleaded with him to be home more and to move out of the city. Timothy knew Frances was a great mother and he wasn't about to question her ability to parent. All he knew was that his baby girl was fighting for her life and that Frances and Ashley needed him now more than ever.

"I'll be there as soon as I can, and I love you." Timothy hung up and went and found Randy. "My daughter was hit by a car and I have to leave. You're in charge again."

"Oh my God, is she going to be all right?" Randy asked.

"I don't know," Timothy said. "All I know is that I have to get there now."

As he raced down the freeway, his mind was full of visions of Ashley. He remembered playing soccer with her the previous week. He remembered her third birthday party, with the cake shaped like Elmo. He remembered holding her for the first time in the hospital and how good he felt that day, and how precious she was to him. His mind was so full he could hardly focus on his driving. The drive was a blur until he pulled up to the hospital, where he prayed as he parked, "Please don't take our daughter from us, please. Let her live. Please let her live."

Frances had also called James, but he hadn't picked up. She left a tearful message: "Ashley was hit by a car and she's in County Hospital. They don't know if she's going to make it. Call me as soon as you can, or come straight down to the hospital."

Timothy ran frantically up to the front desk. "I'm Tim Fletcher. My daughter was hit by a car. Her name is Ashley Fletcher. What's her status?"

The receptionist consulted her computer and said, "She's still in the emergency room area. You can go to the waiting room and the doctors will inform you once they know anything."

Timothy asked, "Can I see her?"

"No, the doctors are with her right now," the woman said. "Have a seat in the waiting room and the doctors will be with you shortly."

Timothy found the waiting room and saw Frances sitting alone in a corner, red-eyed. He ran up to her and asked, "Are you all right?"

Frances stood up and hugged Timothy tightly. "No I'm not all right."

Timothy welcomed her touch. He realized now that he loved her just as he had when they were first married. He knew he could never make up for all he had done to her, but he wanted a chance to try. As she released her hold on him and looked into his eyes, he wished her hug could have come under different circumstances.

"She's still in the emergency room and I haven't heard anything yet. I'm so worried, Tim. I don't know what to do."

"Don't worry," Timothy said. "I'm here for you and I won't leave your side."

They sat down and he asked again, "So what happened?"

Frances began to cry again. "I don't know. Ryan and Ashley went outside to play and the next thing I knew she was lying on the ground bleeding. It was awful seeing her like that." She looked up at him with fear in her eyes; Timothy might easily blame her for what had happened, and after being threatened with reduced visitation rights, Timothy might want revenge. He had changed so much since she had started dating James.

"I know it wasn't your fault," Timothy said. "It's no one's fault. Things happen sometimes and there's no logical answer why they do. You're a great mother and you love Ashley and Ryan deeply. Look what kind of father I've been. I've been horrible. I put my business before you and the kids, thinking everything would be all right. I was a fool and I didn't even see it until it was too late. I'm an awful person and I hate who I was. How could I have been so stupid?"

Frances was surprised, to say the least, at Timothy's admission of guilt. He had never been one to admit he was wrong about anything in the past, and now it sounded as if he was taking all the blame for their failed marriage. *Maybe he has changed. Maybe he knows now that the children are the most important thing in the world.*

"What's important now is Ashley," Timothy said. "Where's Ryan?"

"With Kelly," Frances said. "He'll be fine until my parents arrive tomorrow evening. What about work?"

"Randy took over for me," Timothy said. "He's been doing that a lot for me lately."

Frances was totally bewildered now. *Timothy would have never let anyone run his business before. He* is *different now.*

She took Timothy's hand and said, "I don't know what I'll do if anything happens to Ashley. I don't know if I could go on."

Timothy choked back his tears. "You mustn't talk like that. She's going to be all right. She has to be."

Timothy was just about to tell Frances how he felt about her, and how sorry he was, when an exhausted-looking man in blue scrubs appeared in the doorway and called out, "I'm looking for Frances Fletcher."

"I'm Frances Fletcher," said Frances, standing and approaching him, "and this is my ex-husband Timothy."

"I'm Dr. Kenneth Evans, and I've just come from Ashley. I want to tell you, she's a real fighter. Would you come with me, please?"

Frances and Timothy gasped, suddenly full of hope that Ashley was still alive. They followed Dr. Evans into his office and sat down. The doctor said calmly, "Ashley is still with us right now. She lost a lot of blood and we're doing everything we can to stabilize her. You should know that she's in a coma. She received a major head injury from the impact, and that's our biggest concern. If she hadn't been wearing that helmet we wouldn't even be having this conversation." Frances made the sign of the cross and the doctor continued, "If there is swelling of the brain, that could be extremely serious."

Frances shrieked and said, "No, Doctor, please."

Dr. Evans said, "I promise you, we're doing everything we can for her. When someone is in a coma, one of two things will usually happen: they will wake up in a day or two, or they'll stay out for quite some time. Some may never wake up. I hate to tell you this, but I must let you know exactly what we're looking at."

As Frances and Timothy stared helplessly at him, he continued, "Besides the loss of blood and the head injury, she has a couple other issues we need to be concerned about. She has a shattered pelvis near where the femur and the pelvis attach. Her femur or thigh bone is broken as well. If she does make it, she may never walk again."

"No, Doctor, no," Frances sobbed. Timothy, his eyes full of tears, couldn't speak.

"I wish that was all there was but there's more," Dr. Evans said. "She has a broken arm which will eventually need surgery. It can be mended, but she'll need pins in her forearm to make it heal properly. That's the least of our concerns right now. The head injury and coma are what we really have to worry about."

"What are her chances to make it?" Timothy choked out.

"I can't answer that," said Dr. Evans. "Everyone's different. I can tell you one thing though. As I said, she's a fighter. I've seen people with lesser injuries that gave up and were gone instantly. She's holding on. It always gives us hope when a patient shows such tenacity. We should know more in a day or two."

Frances was still trying to hold herself together. "Can we see her?"

"She's in intensive care right now," Dr. Evans said. "I can arrange for you to see her for a minute or two, but that's it. She won't be able to hear you. I'll have a nurse escort you in a few minutes. If you'll go back to the waiting room, she'll come get you."

Timothy and Frances went back into the waiting room and ten minutes later a nurse came for them. When they walked into Ashley's room, she was lying utterly still on her back; her head was wrapped in bandages. Her leg was up in traction and her arm was immobilized by another contraption.

Swallowing their tears, the two silently approached their child's bed. Frances bent over the pillow and softly said, "I love you, Ashley."

Taking Frances' hand, Timothy said, "It's Daddy. I love you too, Ashley. I know you can hear me. Listen to Daddy. Don't give up. Mommy and Daddy are here for you and won't ever leave your side. When you wake up, we can go get ice cream like we used to. Please don't give up. Mommy and Daddy need you."

The nurse said, "We need to let her be now. She needs all the rest she can get." They nodded, sniffling, and followed the nurse back to the waiting room.

Frances' sadness turned to anger. "Why did this happen to her, Tim? What did she ever do to deserve this? She's five years old! She's so innocent! Why did God allow this?"

Timothy could see that Frances was headed for a breakdown. Remembering what Alexander had said about faith, he said, "Our place is not to question why something happens. Everything happens for a reason. God has plans for each and every one of us."

Frances was stunned. She couldn't believe that Timothy would say that; he had never shown faith before, that she knew of. "You *are* different now," Frances said. "Thank you."

"Thank you for what? I've been a terrible father."

"Thank you for what you said to Ashley and thank you for what you said to me. When I saw her lying there I was so upset I didn't know what to say. It helped me cope when you took over. And… thank you for being her father."

Timothy smiled at Frances. Frances then said, "Thank you for being here with me right now. I don't think I could make it if you weren't here."

Timothy ventured a small smile and said quietly, "I love you, Frances. I'll be here as long as it takes, until Ashley's better. I'll stay by your side the entire time if you need me to."

They spent the evening together in the waiting room in quiet agony. A nurse came up to them just before ten and said, "You two can go home and get some sleep; there's really nothing you can do here. We'll notify you if there's any change in her condition."

"Not a chance," Frances said. "I'm staying here the entire night if I have to. That's my baby in there and I won't leave."

"Me too," Timothy said.

"There's a chapel on the second floor if you need comfort," the nurse said.

"Thank you," Frances said.

After the nurse left Timothy said, "I'll spend twenty nights in a row if I have to here to help our baby girl."

They spent the next hour talking and helping each other cope with what was inevitably going to be the most difficult night of their lives. Finally Timothy said, "I'm going to go to the chapel for a little while. You stay here just in case there's any word on Ashley. If you hear anything, come and get me right away."

"Go ahead," Frances said.

There was no one else in the chapel. Timothy knelt down and prayed, "Alexander help me, please help me. I know you can hear me and I know you're real. Please help me."

Alexander appeared to Timothy. When Timothy looked up and saw Alexander he felt a little better. Timothy said, "Where have you been when I needed you so badly?"

"You needed to work through this on your own," Alexander said.

"Can you help me, Alexander, please?" Timothy pleaded. "Help Ashley pull through."

"I don't have that power," said Alexander. "That's up to one who is much greater than I."

"You're an angel, Alexander, and you're supposed to be able to perform miracles," Timothy said. "Perform a miracle and help Ashley get better. I know you can do it, please."

"I can't control who dies and who lives," Alexander said with genuine regret. "If I could, I would. I can't, Timothy, I just can't."

"No!" Timothy said.

Alexander's words weren't much comfort to the grief-stricken Timothy. Nothing less than knowing that Ashley would be all right would satisfy him, so Alexander left him there to pray.

Once he was alone, Timothy made the greatest act of faith he had ever shown in his life. He prayed, "Please, God, give Frances and me strength to make it through whatever you have planned for Ashley. If it is your will to take her, then do so. I will respect your decision and follow you the rest of my life either way. I'm sorry for all the horrible things I've done. I was blind, but now I see the truth. Thank you for giving me another chance and not giving up on me. Help Ashley with the pain, dear God. She's in so much pain. Please don't let her suffer."

Timothy prayed most of the night until he fell asleep in the pew, exhausted from the trauma. Frances spent the night dozing fitfully in the waiting room.

The next morning Frances woke up first, and went right to the nurses' station. The nurse told her that unfortunately there was no change in Ashley's condition. Having been cooped up all night, Frances decided to go outside for some fresh air.

She walked out of the hospital double doors and down the sidewalk; suddenly she heard a familiar voice from just around the corner. It was James; she started to walk up to him, but then stopped before he saw her.

James was on his cell phone. She heard him say, "Yeah baby, last night was the best. Sure, I'll be over Thursday night. We can do the same again. You were terrific last night. Work is crazy, so I won't be able to call you for a while. I have to go – 'bye."

He had another call coming in and answered it: "Hey baby. I'm sorry I couldn't see you last night. I got tied up with work being so busy and all. Tell you what though, maybe I can come over Tuesday next week and spend the night. I'll bring some wine and we'll have some fun. All right then, Tuesday night." He hung up and put his phone in his pocket.

Frances stood frozen for a moment, then hurried back into the hospital to think about what to do next. *How could I be so stupid? Timothy was right. I should never doubt him again. I almost ruined my life.*

She waited for James inside the entrance of the hospital, disgusted at the type of person he really was, and disgusted that she hadn't seen through his treacherous ways earlier. He walked in, spotted her and said, "Hi, baby, I came right over when I heard what happened. My phone was dead last night. Is Ashley going to be all right?"

Frances said, "Why would you care?"

"What do you mean?"

"I know what you are," Frances said. "I can't believe I almost fell for you! I know you're a no-good cheat!"

"What are you talking about?"

"I was outside a minute ago and heard you talking to two different women. You're a pig! Get out of here and don't ever come back!" She slapped him on the face.

For a moment James looked as if he was going to hit her back; then, instead, he laughed, "Do you think you're the only woman that's ever slapped me? I've had a lot of women a lot prettier than you that couldn't tame me. You're pathetic, you and that psycho husband of yours. I'm glad this happened so now I don't have to pretend I like those bratty kids of yours."

She raised her hand again and James grabbed it. Frances began to cry and said, "I don't ever want to see you again. Get out of here."

"You don't have to worry about that," sneered James. "I wouldn't waste my time on someone like you anyway. I mean, face it. You have two kids! Who's going to want to deal with that type of baggage? You'll be lucky if you ever get a date again." He turned on his heel and strutted away.

Frances was very upset, not about losing James, but about having treated Timothy so badly. She went to find him in the chapel. Timothy had just woken up and was on his knees all alone.

Timothy prayed, "Come to me, Alexander. Please come to me."

Frances was watching discreetly, and wondered, *Who is he praying to?*

Alexander appeared, but Frances couldn't see or hear him. Timothy asked, "Any word on Ashley yet? Is she going to be all right?"

"She is," Alexander said. "You'll have your daughter with you for a long time."

"Thank you, Alexander!" Timothy said. "Thank you so much!"

"Don't thank me," Alexander said. "I had nothing to do with it. I think you know who you need to thank."

"Well, thank you for showing me the right way to live."

Frances stared; it was as if Timothy was talking to no one.

"There is more," Alexander said. "Ashley will live, but she'll have to go through a lot in the next few months and she will need you by her side."

"I won't leave her side once," Timothy said.

"I have to warn you that Ashley will never walk again without a slight limp. She won't be able to play sports like other children and she'll barely be able to keep up with them at times."

"I don't care," Timothy said, "as long as she lives."

"Ashley has the chance to do something greater than anyone in your family has ever done," Alexander said. "Oh, she won't be thought of as a great person in the way that the world views greatness. They rate everyone on how much money they have. In fact, she might even be thought of as a failure in that way. But she does have the chance to live, knowing the true meaning of life. The true meaning of life is to help others, especially children. In heaven you are greatly honored if you spend your entire life helping children. She has the chance to help handicapped children, which is even better."

Suddenly the lights flickered, the air fluttered in the closed room and a piece of paper blew off the table in the corner. Frances gasped and shivered with apprehension.

Alexander raised his eyes to heaven and murmured, "I'm sorry." Then, to Timothy, he explained, "I'm not supposed to reveal anything about the future because it's not set in stone. Ashley will be tempted along the way just as you were. She could choose the wrong path and end up on the other side. Remember our discussion of free will; she'll have many choices to make, but I'm sure with you as her father you can guide her in the right direction."

"What about Ryan?" Timothy asked.

"All I can tell you is you won't be disappointed in him either, if he too can resist temptation. A parent has a lot to do with how a child turns out. You know how good a parent Frances is. Now you have to be equally as good."

"I will," said Timothy, "I promise!"

"There is one other thing," Alexander said. "My opponent won't take this defeat easily; your life is about to change drastically. In time, though, he'll move on and you'll find peace from above. You will face many adversities along the way, my friend. It won't be easy. Remember, your faults have been great and you have a lot to pay for. In time you will despise the life you used to live. You have a chance to be happier than you ever have been before."

"I understand," Timothy said. "Whatever happens, I will face it with a smile. I'm just so happy Ashley's going to be all right."

"Then this is goodbye," Alexander said.

"Thank you, Alexander," Timothy said.

Alexander disappeared. Immediately Timothy prayed, "Thank you, God, for saving my daughter. I promise I will never go down the wrong path again. I promise you I will follow you until the day I die, no matter what happens.

Forgive me for all my trespasses against others and forgive me for my dishonesty.

"Most of all, forgive me for not seeing what a beautiful, loving woman you gave me. I was so stupid and didn't know how great Frances is. I love her with all my heart and I will cherish the ground she walks on if you will give me another chance with her. Please, God, bring her back to me." Timothy stood up and looked up to heaven and said, "I love you and will serve you until my last breath."

Frances was glowing inside. She knew he had changed and was going to be the man she had always wanted. Frances walked up to Timothy and said, "I heard the whole thing. I love you too, Tim. I never stopped loving you."

Timothy took Frances in his arms and hugged her as he hadn't done in a long time, murmuring, "Please forgive me."

Frances looked into Timothy's eyes and said, "I forgive you. I never quit praying for God to send someone to help you. I prayed everyday for that since we were married. I guess prayers are answered. I love you, Timothy."

"I love you, too."

"Timothy – who is Alexander?"

"Well, Franny, you asked God to send someone, and he did. I told you before that a guardian angel came to me; he's the one who helped me see the error of my ways. Thank you for praying for that, Franny — you saved me."

"I will never doubt you again as long as I live," Frances said.

They went back to the waiting room and a few minutes later Dr. Evans came for them. "I have good news. Ashley has come out of her coma. She has a long way to recovery, but I think she's going to make it. I doubt she'll ever walk again though."

"She'll walk again," said Timothy. "You just have to have a little faith."

"We all could use a little of that," said Dr. Evans. "You can go see her now."

Ashley was awake but groggy. She opened her eyes and mumbled, "Hi, Mommy. Hi, Daddy. I was dreaming we all went out for ice cream." Frances' heart fluttered; she glanced at Timothy with a huge lump in her throat. She took his hand and felt even more at peace.

The nurse said, "Save your strength, honey," even as Ashley faded into sleep again. The nurse then said, "She'll be in and out for the next couple of hours. Let her rest. You can see her again in a little while." Timothy and Frances, filled with joy, went back to the waiting room.

A few days later, Ashley underwent surgery to repair her arm and leg. She came through well, though she would need one more operation before they were able to repair her leg well enough for her to be able to try to walk. Timothy and Frances were so thankful that Ashley was alive that they bore the prospect of the long recovery without despair. Their faith would now be what guided them through life.

Timothy finally went back to his office a few weeks later to put his business up for sale. When he arrived there, people were everywhere, going through things in his office. Timothy asked, "What's going on here?"

A man with a badge clipped to his tie walked up and asked, "Are you Timothy Fletcher?"

"Yes."

The man said, "I'm Richard Marks from the Securities and Exchange Commission. These other men are from the FBI. I have a warrant for your arrest, and we have a warrant to search the entire premises. You are under arrest for insider trading in connection with an illegal purchase of a stock called Dataware. All your assets are frozen."

Timothy laughed sadly to himself. *Alexander said I'd be sorry if I made that trade. I guess he was right.* He turned to Randy and said, "Call John Jacobs, my attorney."

"Already called him, sir," said Randy.

Timothy pled guilty to insider trading. John wanted him to fight it, but Timothy had meant what he had said about taking his punishment with a smile. He was sentenced to eighteen months in federal prison, given a seventy-five thousand dollar fine, and had his license to trade securities revoked. The company went bankrupt. He was even publically humiliated when his picture appeared on a national business magazine with the headline *Does Your Broker Trade Illegally?*

He served a little less than a year in prison. Frances knew what was in Timothy's heart and waited for him without complaint. She had closed on the farm in Wisconsin before Ashley's accident and the SEC didn't move on it because the farm was in her name.

When Timothy was released, the family moved to Wisconsin and worked the dairy farm as Timothy's family had done for generations. He raised his children to be followers of God and taught them the difference between right and wrong. Frances was able to go back to teaching after Ryan and Ashley had gotten a little older.

Timothy prayed every day, thanking God when he got up in the morning and before he went to bed at night. He never forgot once what had happened to him. He was a changed man, focused and honest. He lived his life on faith and never forgot about the evils of temptation.

A voice boomed from the depths of hell: "George Samuels, report at once." When Samuels reported, the voice said, "I'm disappointed in your last assignment. You underestimated that man. Your streak is over. You have another assignment, and this time you must not fail. His name is Kenneth Campbell. Review his life and get ready to steal his soul."

Samuels cried, "This one will not get away!"

"You will pay a high price if he does," boomed the voice.

A voice in heaven rang out: "Alexander Hargrove, report to your superior."

Alexander appeared before Andrew, who congratulated him. "You performed heroically on your last mission. Many angels are talking about how you stopped Samuels' streak."

"Thank you," Alexander said, bowing low.

"Here is your next assignment," said Andrew. "His name is Kenneth Campbell. Review his life and get ready to secure his soul."

And so the fight in heaven and hell raged on, with Samuels and Alexander pitted against each other once again.